Fragments of the Past

Paperback Version

Historical Fiction Stories

By Angelia

CONTENTS

Taryn Pearl

Chapter 1

here are stories told for a specific reason: to be a monitor to those who listen or read them and not to forget the past times, which our own times have come from. Therefore, the reader may forgive some inaccuracies or lingerings in the story and focus on the tale's moral.

It must be remarked that, at the end of the eighteenth century,, the Society considered coercion of women to force them to marriage acceptable. Many women got married in this way at that time.

In Ireland, where our scene is set, the Church tried discouraging this attitude, but with poor results.

Even some local noblemen used this method, so it is not surprising that a young, good-looking lady, like this story's main character, caught some men's eyes. Taryn Pearl was from a middle-upper-class family from Enniscorthy, and she was the last child. In the spring of 1795, she had just turned seventeen.

Her brothers and sisters were all married, and she had begun to receive her first suitors. Among the suitors was Sir Frederick Montrose, who was from one of the most ancient noble families in the area; nevertheless, the Pearls were hesitating about his proposal, as he had the reputation of being unreliable.

With his pride wounded by the suspected refusal, the Squire Montrose decided to have Taryn all the same, and he carried out his nefarious plan to attempt her honor.

He had the opportunity when he met her by chance in a park while she was walking in the company of another young lady. While the two ladies were leaving the park, Sir Frederick's servant, sent by him, blocked Taryn and forced her into the nobleman's carriage.

Frightened, her friend tried to get some help, but the carriage sped away. Now, the reader might imagine Taryn's apprehension at being dragged away by strangers, and all the more when she was taken to an isolated country manor.

In the anxiety of the moment, Taryn did not recognize Sir Frederick. After all, she had met him once only. After her repeated requests for explanations, he finally answered, declaring himself.

"I remember Your Lordship," she said. "What is the reason

for such a vile act? What do you want from me?"

"Making you my wife," he replied.

"But my family…," Taryn muttered in confusion.

"We don't need your family's consent."

"This is not the behavior of a decent gentleman!"

"Sometimes radical means are necessary."

"Please let me go home," she asked, frightened, but Sir Frederick didn't listen to her.

In the house, some servants and a pair of maids were present; one of them brought Taryn a glass of water.

After a while, Taryn began to feel unwell, but it wasn't just because of the anxiety: to carry out his lecherous plans, Sir Frederick had put a drug the water. Taryn fainted, and later, she recovered after about two hours, waking in a bedroom, in pain and bleeding.

Taryn could not remember anything about what had happened, and she didn't have the experience to understand, but a maid, helping her to take a bath, explained to her what the bleeding meant. Taryn could not believe the crime committed by Sir Frederick and broke into tears from desperation.

She felt overwhelmed by shame; a thousand thoughts came to her mind. How would she explain it to her family? Would they think badly of her, believing she had consented? The thought of telling them grieved her heart.

Taryn was also afraid that Montrose would return and repeat his villainous act, despite the maid trying to reassure her by telling that Squire Montrose had honorable intentions regarding her.

In the meantime, Taryn's friend had gone to the Pearls to tell them about the happening, and, having recognized Lord Montrose's carriage, she directed them towards the nobleman. Concerned, Mr. and Mrs. Pearl went to Montrose hall, suspecting already what the purpose of the abduction was. Sir Frederick had returned home meanwhile, and he received them.

"We are here because of a communication concerning our daughter, overly dafaming to be believed, but it was our duty to verify it," Sir Sidney Pearl said to him.

"Defaming?" Sir Frederick asked in annoyance. "Is it not natural for someone in my position to want a maiden as a wife?"

"It is not decorous to attempt a maiden's honor or marry her without the family's consent!"

"In this case, allow me to make amends for my reckless act by making thy daughter an honest woman."

The Pearls were outraged by the nobleman's arrogance.

"Where is she?" asked Sir Sidney.

"She is not here."

"I demand to see my daughter immediately!"

"I shall let you see her."

"And I hope to find her healthy and honest!" Sir Sidney remarked severely.

Sir Frederick did not answer to the last sentence. He sent for his servant at his country estate asking him to bring Taryn to his home.

Sir Frederick told the Pearls to return in two hours to see Taryn. As soon as the servant received Sir Frederick's message, he told Taryn he was asked to bring her back to the town to meet her family. She felt relieved on the one hand, but on the other hand, she was troubled and ashamed to meet her folks. She could not find in her mind the right words to explain what had happened.

When she arrived at Montrose hall, she found Mr. and Mrs. Pearl waiting for her. As soon as she saw them, she broke into tears.

"I swear I am innocent! I have never encouraged Lord Montrose!"

Her mother held her and reassured her.

"I know you haven't." Then she asked, whispering to her: "Only tell me if it is too late."

Taryn did not know what to say, but Sir Frederick

addressed them.

"You should be grateful I intend to make your daughter my wife. I could leave her dishonored, but I am a righteous man."

"I have never consented to become his wife," Taryn said agitated,:

"Thy daughter and I are de facto husband and wife," Sir Frederick continued "Therefore, it must be only formalized."

Mr. and Mrs. Pearl were insulted by Sir Frederick's words.

"Thee dared to take advantage of a decent lady?!" Sir Sidney shouted. "Thee are a man with no honor!"

"Sir, given me understanding your perturbed mood I tolerate your offense, but be careful with your words," Sir Frederick said to him.

Mrs. Pearl hugged Taryn with teary eyes.

"We'll take you home," she said with a low voice.

"Thy daughter is not going anywhere until we'll be officialized our union," Sir Frederick stated.

"What?" muttered Mrs. Pearl.

"You need not worry about her; she will be treated as my wife," Sir Frederick said.

The Pearls knew, with a daughter dishonored, they had no choice but to condescend.

"On these terms, I accept the marriage," Sir Sidney said.

"What did you say?" she asked her father in dismay.

"You are dishonored," he said to her.

Taryn tried to address to her mother, but she interrupted.

"Nobody else will marry you."

"You cannot give me in marriage to this monster!" Taryn exclaimed in indignation.

"She will stay in the house I have prepared for her until the wedding day," Sir Frederick intervened.

"You cannot prevent me from going home!" Taryn said, standing up to him.

"You are already my wife to all intents and purposes," he replied, ordering the servant to take her back to the manor.

He dragged her away, while she begged her parents to intervene; Mrs. Pearl began to cary, resigned giving her daughter to Sir Frederick.

When the Pearls returned home, Sir Sidney spoke to his wife.

"Lord Montrose is willing to marry her. It could have been worse. After all, he is a respectable nobleman."

Mrs. Pearl said nothing; she was just saddened for Taryn being far away after all she had been through.

Taryn was brought back to Sir Frederick's estate, distressed about what could happen to her. She spent all the night crying, and she promised herself she would never let Sir Frederick touch her again.

Could the reader imagine the grief that was afflicting Taryn for being a prisoner in that house, on her own, far from her family? And her suffering about her honor lost and being deprived of her hopes for the future?

When Sir Frederick went to visit her the following day, she felt a twinge of disrelish in her chest at the idea of meeting him again.

"I wanted to assure you will have everything you need," Sir Frederick said to her. "If you have any request, you can make it to the servants. You will also have a personal maid",

"Please Sir, I only wish to return to my family. Can you not make an act of compassion in my regard?"

"Your family is me now and the children we shall have."

"I do not intend to accept Thee as a husband!" Taryn said in indignanation.

"You have no choice. Besides, I will not be visiting you until the wedding day."

"I will never give an answer at the altar!" "Do not test my patience!" Sir Frederick yelled at her in annoyance. "Haven't you been educated to obey and stay in your place?"

"I have not been educated to deal with beasts!"

"How dare you talk to me in that way?"

"I feel only scorn for you!" she turned her back to him and walked upstairs.

Taryn thought she would have fled from there, but it wasn't easy because she was watched by the servants and was locked in her room during the night.

She tried to think of a way to do it, but even if she would have managed, how would she have reached the town? How would she have become orientated in those country roads?

Taryn felt overwhelmed by distress, and she prayed intensely for the strength and the wisdom she needed to get out of that situation.

□

Chapter 2

The following day, Taryn expressed to the servants the wish to have Confession. They had a message delivered to Sir Frederick, and he replied telling to send forthe Parish of the nearby Church.

Taryn she knew she was not to blame for what had happened to her, but she still felt the necessity to confess the happening.

In the afternoon, the Priest went to the manor, and Taryn received him In confession, she claimed her innocence, and she asked for advice about her situation.

"What have I done to attract such lascivious desires?"

The Priest reassured her she had nothing to be blamed for and encouraged her not to give into misery. However, he added that she should consider the marriage to the Squire Montrose, to repair her condition.

Taryn meant not to follow the advice and she asked the servants the permission to correspond with her family. Delivering the message to Sir Frederick, the servants obtained his permission, on the condition that Taryn would not write directions or references about her whereabouts.

So Taryn wrote a letter to her family, declaring again her

innocence and begging them not to give her in marriage to Sir Frederick.

That day Taryn refused the meals; her stomach was closed. After the maid's insistence, she forced herself to swallow a few spoonfuls of soup. Then the maid offered to accompany her on a walk in the garden to let her get some fresh air. As they walked Taryn saw a gentleman riding on the driveway and, stopping to speak to a servant, she asked the maid who that gentleman was.

"He is Squire Montrose's cousin," she replied. "Sometimes he comes to visit."

Taryn just saw him from afar before the maid led her back into the house. The reply letter from the Pearls arrived the following day:

"Dearest daughter, your loving parents have never doubted your innocence. Our hearts ache as much as yours because of your situation. If there was a way to avoid this marriage, we would have tried it, but a maiden's dishonor is a misfortune that precludes the possibility of another marriage. We wish to spare you the life of loneliness and outcasting reserved for 'fallen women'. The Squire Montrose can guarantee a lavish and respectable life to you. What we do is solely in your interest. May our prayers give you strength while we are waiting to meet again".

Taryn was disappointed, for her parents didn't care about her feelings, that she should have spent her life alongside a man who had caused her suffering and who she despised.

Not giving into, Taryn wrote a reply letter to her parents telling she would have rather take the vows.

Although Taryn always wanted to have a family, the religious life seemed more bearable than a life with Montrose.

Taryn had been spending her days mostly in her room; twice in a day, the maid took her for walks in the garden.

She had lost her appetite, and she used to eat very little.

The maid had brought her some books as a distraction, but Taryn could not think of anything but to break free from Montrose.

In the meantime, the Squire Montrose had given instructions to the maids to sew Taryn's wedding dress. Sir Frederick was more taken with her, and he thought she 'belonged' to him after he had taken her honor.

Taryn felt like a bird locked in a cage, and she spent nights in self-pitying and praying. She had always dreamed of marrying and having a family, but now all that had been stolen from her. She had become another 'fallen woman'; a misfortune that all women tried to avoid.

Every night, she raised a supplication:

"My Lord, do not leave me at the mercy of this man's

yearning. Give me the strength to resist overbearingness and to keep my conscience clean. Bestow me the sapience to understand what to do and to put it into practice. Grant me justice for the wrong done to me."

She wrote another letter to her parents, remarking that she would never answer at the altar and about her decision to undertake the religious life.

She gave the letter to the maid telling her: "Make sure they'll receive it by tomorrow, please."

"As you command, milady. Matthew is going to town tomorrow. Is the dress to your liking?"

"How could something representing my confinement be in my liking? And you, how can you be an accomplice to such an ignoble act?"

"I am just a subordinate; I obey, milady."

"I know you are not to blame. But please, do not make it harder for me", Taryn said before walking back into her room.

The following day, Taryn received her parents's letter, which was not the response she had expected from them:

"Dearest daughter, we understand your disappointment about our decision. However, we'd rather have a well-married daughter than a daughter devoted to the monastic life. The Squire Montrose, with all his faults, is a respectable nobleman, and he is not worse than other nobles in town.

Besides, you have not thought about the wags. You and consequently our family might be the object of rumors if we provoked Lord Montrose's wrath with a refusal. Therefore we ask you to use your senses and to do the right thing. Your loving parents."

On the one hand, Taryn understood their reasons, but she meant not to give herself to Lord Montrose.

She wrote a letter in reply:

"As a daughter who loves and respects her family, the last thing I would want is bringing shame. But I cannot help but wonder why I have to be condemned for years to come for something I am not to blame for! And to spend my life alongside a man who caused me so much grief and every day would remind me what I have been through! What have I done to deserve such a misfortune? I have always obeyed my family and the dictates of ethics. I have nurtured the virtues as best as I could.

"I have never offended or given reason for complaining to my family. I beg you to understand that I am opposing this marriage solely to preserve my self-respect. I understand your concerns, and I do not blame you for them.

But how could I let Lord Montrose touch me again? How could I pretend to respect him as I'm supposed to respect a spouse if I only feel disdain for him? Should I be dishonest with someone I have to oath loyalty to? If you love me, release me from this disgrace! Your devoted daughter."

However, Taryn had no have time to send the letter because she fell ill with a fever that evening.

It was probably the stress she had been through that made her fall ill. The maids assisted her and alerted Sir Frederick, who sent a doctor to visit her.

Thanks to the doctor's treatment, the fever broke down after two days, although Taryn had lost weight and was still weak.

On the fifth day someone came to the manor: from the window Taryn recognized the horse belonging to Sir Frederick's cousin.

She went downstairs and she found him there, a tall young man with clear hair, definitely good-looking and with a proud bearing. He was surprised to see Taryn and greeted her.

"I did not know there was a guest,", he said to her.

"Miss Pearl is Lord Montrose's guest," the servant replied.

'Guest': a word was never less pertinent!

"Jude Montrose," the gentleman said, kissing her hand.

"Delighted," she muttered, and then added, "Taryn Pearl."

"Pearl… are you related to Sir Sidney Pearl?"

"Yes, Sir, he is my father."

"I met him years ago." After giving instructions to the

servant, Mr. Montrose took his leave.

Outside he exchanged a few words with one of the maid.

"Miss Pearl is a gentlewoman. Is she betrothed to my cousin?"

"Yes, she is, Sir."

"And why is she here unaccompanied?"

"I believe you should ask this question to Lord Montrose, Sir."

As he left the estate, Jude Montrose had suspicions about Taryn's presence there since he knew the noblemen's custom.

Given his thoughts on the matter, he decided to return to the manor the following day in the evening. He made an excuse to the servants to justify his presence. He found Taryn in the living room and greeted her.

"I often come to the manor to go hunting," he said, "I hope my presence is not a nuisance for Your Ladyship."

"Absolutely not, Sir."

"I beg your pardon, but I see you are very pale. Maybe you should go outside."

Taryn's maid intervened.

"I was about to take Miss Pearl for a walk in the garden."

"I can accompany her, since I am leaving," he replied to her.

Taryn felt uncomfortable to go out with him alone.

"Well, it's getting dark...", she said.

"There is fresh air outside; it will be good for you," Jude said, his manners reassuring to Taryn.

She and the gentleman walked out to the back of the house while the maid was watching them from the window.

"Forgive my intrusion," he said to her, "but I could not help but notice Thy uneasiness, or perhaps it is just my impression..."

Taryn did not know what to answer.

"How long have you been here?" Jude asked.

"Six days," she replied as they stopped.

"Are you here against your will?" Jude asked. Taryn looked down nervously.

"Lord Montrose, he wants me to marry him," she muttered.

"And Thy family?" he asked; Taryn did not answer. "So it is true, Thee are being held against your will? I shall go and tell your family."

"But Lord Montrose..." she interrupted, surprised by his words.

"I shall deal with him," Jude affirmed.

"Why would you do that?" she asked in confusion.

"Because I do not think this is right," he replied. They walked on, not to arouse suspicion in the maid.

"My family is aware that Lord Montrose brought me here," Taryn said.

"Are they aware?"

"They had no choice but to accept the marriage. But I am living in fear and in distress."

"I shall speak to Thy family," Jude said, having mercy for her.

"It is not necessary," Taryn said as they stopped. "Just help me get out of here. I am watched day and night."

"Thee will hearfrom me soon. Now go back inside, or they may become suspicious", Jude suggested.

"Thank you, Sir," Taryn said, impressed by him. "May the Lord reward you for Thy generosity." She walked back to the house, trying to hide her emotion.

Taryn was so relieved to have found help, and from the most unexpected person. Besides, Taryn thought that fleeing was not the only problem to solve: even if she would have returned to her folks, who would be certain they would not decide to push her to marry the Squire Montrose?

She feared her endeavors would have been useless.

Meanwhile, Jude Montrose was thinking about a way to take her away. The difficult part was not getting her out of there, but journeying on. They could not use the carriage, so he had to take her on an horse, but the servants certainly would have chased them if they have heard them.

Jude was ashamed of what his cousin had done, but yet he wanted to try to talk sense into him, hoping to appeal to his common   sense.

Chapter 3

Jude went to Montrose hall, and he was received by Sir Frederick.

"Dear cousin, how do you do?" he said.

"I am fine. I have something to discuss with you," Jude replied.

"I am listening",

"In the last days I went hunting on our family's countryside property. And I have been in the manor, where I was received by your servants…",

"Get to the point," Sir Frederick said, sensing already what his cousin was referring to.

"I met Miss Pearl."

"She is my betrothed."

"I was told that. I met her father years ago. She is a good family lady, and I would find it deplorable if anything bad happened to her."

"As I said, we are to marry."

"So she is in a property of yours out of the town of her own will?"

"What exactly are you worried about? That is the way it had always worked," Sir Frederick said, annoyed. "She will be my wife in a few days, and all will be sorted, with her family's consent."

"And what about her? Because she looked quite intimidated to me."

"Her consent is not required."

"You should have a care for your future wife."

"Why are you so concerned about her? You don't even know her."

"Am I asking too much if I demand respect for a lady? You are holding her away from her family against her will."

"The tone you are using is out of turn. Should I remind you that you are in my own home?" Sir Frederick said, irritated.

"Why don't you let her go back to her family?"

"Because de facto, we are already husband and wife."

Jude was bewildered.

"I would have never expected such a baseness by you!" he said indignantly.

"This time, I shall tolerate your offenses because of our blood bond. But keep your distance from Miss Pearl, or I will forget our kinship," Sir Frederick said in a threatening tone.

Jude left Sir Frederick's manor even more determined to get Taryn out of that regrettable situation.

Meanwhile, Taryn was eager to hear from him.

The wedding dress was almost done. That day, while the

maid made the finishings, she consulted Taryn.

"Why are you so upset, milady? Maidens should be pleased when they get married."

"Pleased? How could I be pleased of such a wrong in my regards?"

"The Squire Montrose is from an important family."

"Do you believe I care about family? After what he did to me?"

"Milady, Thee are neither the first nor the last. And it was even worse for some ladies: they were dishonored by someone who refused to marry them. The Squire Montrose is acting correctly. Our lives don't belong to us." The last sentence upset Taryn even more.

She had heard about some 'fallen women', who had been outcasts from Society, but she would have never suspected to have the same fate as them! She was tormented thinking she could no longer get married or have a family. She was oppressed in body and spirit for the wrong done to her. Her only hope to avoid the marriage with Squire Montrose laid in Jude Montrose now.

During the afternoon, she saw him arriving at the manor. She went downstairs, where he was speaking to the servants giving instructions. He greeted her and showed her a book he was holding.

"The other day I promised to Miss Pearl to lend her a book she would like to read. It will be a distraction to her for the time she will be here."

Taryn realized the book was a message from him. She took it and thanked him.

She waited until he was gone, then she went upstairs and opened the book, in it she found a note:

"Your Ladyship, we must act as soon as possible to get you out of there. If Thee are seriously determined not to marry my cousin, I shall come back tomorrow to speak to you.

"The road leading to the town is about a kilometer long. Using the carriage would call the servants' attention. Therefore, if you are able to ride, it will be better to use the horses.

"It must be done in the night. I have also thought of a way to get you out of the house. Thee will receive my visit tomorrow morning.

"God bless you. Thy Servant, Jude Montrose".

Jude's letter had raised Taryn's hopes.

Regarding the matter of her family, Taryn had thought it would be better to go straight to the monastery and ask for asylum there.

In the evening, Taryn conversed with the maid as she helped her brush her hair.

"How long have you known the Montroses?" Taryn asked.

"I have been at service of the Montrose family since the Lords, Sir Frederick's folks, were living."

"So you know Lord Montrose's cousin either? Do you know him well?"

"I know him enough."

"Is he married?"

"No, he is not. Why do you ask, milady?"

"He has just aroused my curiosity."

"Thee should be more interested in your betrothed."

"Do not mention him again!" Taryn said, displeased.

"He is going to be Thy husband, milady."

"Should I give my body to a man who doesn't mind ruining someone's life just for a whim?" Taryn asked in annoyance. "May the heaven save me from such husbands!"

"If you continue with this behavior, Thee are going to provoke his wrath, milady," Taryn did not answer and she went to bed.

The following morning, Jude returned to the manor. Going downstairs, Taryn greeted him.

"Good morning, Miss Pearl," he said to her, then he addressed the servants. "The other day, Miss Pearl had expressed the wish to see the rabbits. I have offered to accompany her."

The maid had nothing against that. Jude and Taryn walked to the back of the house as the maid watched them from the window.

"I thank you again for what Your Lordship is doing for me," Taryn said to him.

"Are you convinced to do this?"

"Without any doubt." They reached the shed with the rabbit cages. "Besides, I can ride."

Jude opened a cage and took a bunny.

"Take it," he gave it to Taryn.

"He is adorable," Taryn commented as she caressed the little animal.

"Have you thought about your future? Are you aware Thee may not be able to get married anymore?"

"I am. Indeed. I do not want to be taken back to my family's home, but I prefer to go to a monastery where I can undertake the religious life."

"A monastery?"

"If I return to my family, I still might be pressured to marry the Squire Montrose."

"I am sad for the wrong my cousin has done to you. I have spoken about that with him…"

"Did you really speak to him about it?" Taryn asked, surprised.

"Yes, I did. But I didn't let him suspect anything. He has confided in me... what happened," Jude replied in awe., Taryn was embarrassed. "Thee are an incredibly strong lady."

"The Squire Montrose planned my ruin!" Taryn said, hardly holding back the tears. "And by doing it he has deprived me of my future! But Thee had mercy for me. Heaven sent you to me, Sir."

Jude said nothing. He took the bunny from Taryn's hands.

"Thee will hear from me very soon," he said, before walking her back to her house.

Taryn was hopeful, but at the same time, she was worried about escaping. When she saw Sir Frederick's carriage arriving that afternoon, she had a lump in her throat.

Sir Frederick conversed with the servants and asked them if his cousin had been there lately.

"Yes, Sir, he was here this morning," one servant replied.

"If he comes again, I do not want him to be left conversing with Miss Pearl. Am I making myself clear?"

"Yes, Sir," Sir Frederick said, and then he sent for Taryn.

Walking into the room, Taryn spoke to him.

"Sir, I have nothing to converse with Thee, and Thy presence is displeasing to me."

"You will have to become accustomed to it and be pleased by it, since you are about to become my wife."

"I would become Thy wife if I would accept Thee at the altar, but it will never happen."

"I am losing my patience, and if I were you, I would take it seriously!" Montrose said, irritated.

"Your intimidations leave me cold. You cannot deprive me of more than you already did!"

"Don't you understand I did all this to be with you? Your family should not have prevented us from marrying just for futility."

"Do you really think you can justify your behavior?" Taryn said indignantly.

"Your judgments don't affect me," he said. "Besides, I have come to let you know that I have spoken to the Priest of the Church nearby, and I have set a date for the wedding. I thought it would be better to get married in the local Church. The date is the day after tomorrow."

Taryn was dismayed. Sir Frederick did not give her time to answer, and he turned his back, leaving the house.

Time was pressing; she and Jude had to act immediately. The reader might imagine Taryn's anguish in attempting such a risky escape; riding in the countryside in the night, Taryn might have fallen and gotten injured. Other servants might have caught them.

That night, Taryn prayed intensely for being protected

during the escape. She wrote a note for Jude Montrose, and she put it in the book he had given her; she planned to send a servant to deliver the book, but it wasn't necessary. The following morning Jude arrived at the manor.

Taryn went downstairs to greet him, but the servant admonished her.

"The Squire Montrose has given orders for you not to converse with his cousin."

Taryn and Jude were surprised.

"Forgive me, Sir", the servant added, but Taryn replied instead.

"I only came to give back the book Mr. Montrose has lent me." Taryn handed him the book. "Thank you, Sir. I liked it," she said before taking her leave and walking back upstairs.

The note stated:

"Your Lordship,

The Squire Montrose has been in the manor today, and he has informed me he has set the date for the wedding for the day after tomorrow.

I await your instructions, keeping myself ready.

With gratitude and respect,

Thy humble Servant,

Taryn Pearl".

After reading the note, Jude planned to take Taryn away

the following night. He agreed with two of his most trusted servants they should escort him, as in case of necessity they would have held Sir Frederick's servants.

The following morning, a Priest arrived at the manor, coming to bless the houses in the neighborhood.

The servants received him in the house.

"I am the Parish of the near Church," he said to the servants. "Are the Lords at home?"

"No, Father. This manor belongs to Squire Montrose, but he does not live here," a servant replied.

After blessing the house, the Priest spoke to them again.

"Does anyone need to have the Confession?"

"I had my Confession yesterday, Father," a maid replied.

"Is anybody else in the house? It seemed to me to have seen a lady at the window."

"She is Squire Montrose's wife," the servant replied. "She may wish to confess." The maid sent for her.

Given Taryn needed to have the Confession, she went downstairs.

"Good morning, milady," the Priest said.

"Good morning, Father."

"I am offering the blessing to the houses in the neighborhood. I wanted to ask if you would like to have the Confession."

"I would, Father. Thank you." The servants left them alone.

When Taryn knelt down, the Priest gave her a Bible.

"This is from Lord Jude Montrose," he said with a low voice.

"Did he send Your Lordship?" Taryn asked, bewildered. The Priest nodded, and then he confessed her.

Taryn confessed her situation and what had happened to her.

When he left, Taryn went to her room and opened the Bible, finding Jude's note.

"Respectable Miss Pearl, we must act tonight. Be ready; I shall be there along with my servants by 11pm.

I will throw a rope at you, and I will climb up to your room, then we will use a ladder to climb down.

Then we will ride until we will be reached the town, where I shall take you to the nearest monastery.

May the Lord protect you.

Thy Servant,

Jude Montrose".

Taryn followed Jude's instructions: that night, when the maid left the room, she waited for the servants to retire to their rooms (eavesdropping the noises downstairs), and then she got dressed.

She nervously waited for Jude's arrival at the window.

Finally, her deliverance was near.

Chapter 4

Near the manor, Jude and his servants left the horses and walked towards the house, not to call the servants's attention.

Taryn saw them coming through the window. She held her breath agitated; she opened the window and Jude, whispering, told her to tie the rope to something stable and then he threw it to her.

Taryn tied the rope tightly to a closet's foot and then she held it with the hands as Jude climbed up.

Reaching the window, Jude entered, and he gave Taryn a coat.

"Here. It is cold outside," he said to her.

"Thank you", she replied, and she put on the coat on.

Jude unrolled the ladder and tied it to the windowsill.

He helped Taryn get on.

"It will be fine," he said. Taryn climbed down, step by step slowly, and a servant helped her get down. Taryn was relieved.

"The horses are some further," the servant said to her with a low voice.

Jude climbed down, and then they walked fast to the road.

Arriving at the horses, they got on and rode off, first slowly and then quickening their pace; the air was bitter cold that evening.

"Are you all right?" Jude asked Taryn. She nodded, "We should hurry. Do you think you can keep up?"

"I can," Taryn replied.

They rode faster and kept going off the road to avoid being followed, in case the servants knew about Taryn's absence.

After about ten minutes, they sighted the town and slowed down to rest a little. When they arrived in town, Taryn was very weary. Jude proposed her to spend the night in his house since it was closer than the monastery. In the morning, he would take her to the monastery. Although Taryn was uncomfortable about spending the night in Jude's house, she was too tired to refuse.

So they arrived at Montrose mansion and Jude entrusted her to a maid.

"Thank you for all you have done for me, Sir," Taryn said to him before retiring to the room prepared for her.

At dawn, the servants in the manor became aware of Taryn's escape, and they figured out that someone had helped her. They immediately sent news to the Squire Montrose, and he rushed to the manor. He questioned the servants.

"How can it be possible she has escaped?" he asked furiously.

"She has been locked in the room, as usual, Your Lordship," a maid claimed quickly. "Someone has helped her to escape by using a ladder."

Sir Frederick did not take long to figure out who could have been responsible for that. Infuriated, he returned to town, determined to confront Jude.

Meanwhile, Taryn woke, and she went downstairs to have some food. Jude was waiting for her at the table.

"Good morning, Miss Pearl," he said to her.

"Good morning."

"Did you sleep well?"

"Aye," Taryn sat down.

"We can go after breakfast," Jude said.

"Fine," she replied, beginning to eat.

"Forgive my question. I know it is not a concern of mine, but are you determined to go to the monastery?"

"As I said, my family still might pressure me to marry Sir Frederick."

"I understand. But life in a monastery is quite tough."

"What alternative do I have if I can no longer get married?"

"Thee have never considered marrying my cousin, have you?"

"Sir Frederick has already taken my virtue by force. I would have never let him take my dignity too."

"Thee are very courageous, milady," Jude said, before hearing the door bell. Jude stood up, with concerned eyes. "Forgive me, but it is better for you to go upstairs,, he told Taryn and left the room.

The servant announced Sir Frederick's visit to Jude, which he had expected. Jude received him.

"What do I owe your visit to, dear cousin?" Jude asked.

"Don't you pretend with me! I know it was you," said Sir Frederick with an irritated tone. "You helped Miss Pearl to escape."

"I don't even deny it. But she is not here, if that is what you came for. I have brought her to a monastery under her own request."

"A monastery?" asked Sir Frederick, astonished.

"Yes. Miss Pearl decided to undertake a religious life".

"Did you do it without consulting her family first?"

"I could not deny it to her."

"How dare you turn against me? Sneaking in my property as a thief to steal my betrothed!" Sir Frederick said furiously.

"I behaved according to my conscience. Do you think what you have done qualifies you as a good husband? How can you be a good husband if you don't respect your own betrothed?"

"Watch your words!"

"Yours are mere concupiscence",

"I have warned you to stay away from her! But if you think you have stolen her from me, you are wrong. You did it in vain." Saying that, he left the house.

Taryn had recognized Sir Frederick's voice, and she was concerned, but Jude went to reassure her.

"It was predictable he would have understood it was me helping you", he said. "But I told him you weren't here because I had taken you to a monastery already, and he has believed it."

"You have stood up to a kin of yours to help me. Anyone else other than you would not have done it."

"I never approved such 'means' to force women to marriage. And I grieve for the pain my cousin has caused you."

"I hope you can find your own spouse pretty soon," Taryn said with admiration. "Any woman would be honored to be by your side."

Jude nodded and took his leave.

Before taking Taryn to the monastery, Jude exchanged a few words with his maid about her.

"It is absurd that a young lady with her qualities has to live shut in a monastery," Jude commented.

"Miss Pearl seems convinced of her decision," the maid said.

"Should she pay for Frederick's debauchery?!" Jude exclaimed.

He knew Taryn was still in a risky position. Sir Frederick was still a threat to her.

Indeed, Sir Frederick had gone to the Pearls to inform them about Taryn's escape. Astonished by the news, the Pearls learned about Jude Montrose's involvement in her escape. Sir Frederick remarked on his decision to repair her honor by marrying her.

"Try to discover what monastery she is in before I decide to step back and leave her dishonored!" he told them.

Worried, the Pearls went to Montrose mansion.

Meanwhile, Taryn was preparing to go to the monastery; Jude went to converse with her.

"There is something I wish to ask you...", Jude said with a serious look. "Would you be willing to be my wife?"

Taryn was stunned.

"Your wife?" she muttered.

"I am not going to pressure you in any way. I just want you to consider it," Jude affirmed. In awe, Taryn spoke hesitantly.

"But you know that I...", she interrupted.

"Your condition does not matter to me," he said. "You possess qualities that I have rarely seen in others."

Taryn was impressed, and she admired his honor.

"You don't have to give me your answer now," he added. "I will take you to the monastery if Thee wish to."

Taryn said nothing. Jude took his leave, and she, rejoicing, shed some emotional tears.

She believed it wasn't possible for a gentleman to put conventions aside and accept a maid who had been already like kin to him.

Taryn was resigned to renounce marriage, but Jude was offering her the opportunity to live the life she had always desired. What seemed lost was again in her reach.

No words could ever express Taryn's joy and relief.

When she saw her family's carriage from the window, she went downstairs where she found Mr. and Mrs. Pearl conversing with Jude.

"We had a communication regarding our daughter, Taryn, betrothed to Thy kin, the Squire Montrose," Sir Sidney said to Jude. "Accordingly to the communication, she is in a monastery, escorted there by you, under her request."

"Yes, it is so."

"So is it true that Your Lordship stole her from her betrothed?"

"A betrothed who has dishonored her and imposed to her with violence."

"With all due respect, Sir, this is a matter concerning your family and the Squire Montrose only. Now we would like to know which monastery she is in."

Jude was about to answer, but Taryn entered the room at that moment.

"I am here, father," she said. The Pearls were surprised to see her there.

"We were told you were in a monastery," Sir Sidney said.

"It was my intention to go to a monastery."

"You have fled from your betrothed, and now you lodge in the house of a gentleman? Didn't you think your parents had suffered enough?"

"It was not my intention to cause you any concern or shame. Forgive me. But I had to act as my conscience commanded to me," Taryn then addressed Jude. "If you are still willing to do what you proposed to me, I accept."

Jude was glad to hear that.

"What does it mean?", asked Sir Sidney.

"I intend to marry your daughter," Jude said to him. The Pearls were astonished.

"You?" asked Sir Sidney.

"I guarantee to Thy daughter a respectable life. I am not like my cousin," Jude said.

"But Taryn... she..." Sir Sidney started saying in hesitation and awe.

"I am aware of the events occurred and Thy daughter's condition," Jude interrupted, anticipating him. "And I agree to marry her despite all."

The Pearl were speechless.

"To guarantee my commitment, I am willing to ask for a special dispensation *[1] for the wedding even tomorrow."

Jude astounded the Pearls. At those terms, they agreed to the wedding. Taryn was joyful, and she hugged her mother.

Jude insisted that the Pearls and Taryn be guests in his house until the wedding day. Then he sent a missive to Sir Frederick to communicate his engagement to Taryn. Sir Frederick rushed to Montrose mansion.

Furious, he asked Jude for clarification.

"Should I add more that I already told you in the missive? Miss Pearl and I are going to get married," Jude said.

"Now I see the reason why you helped her! You had plans for her, and you wanted to steal her from me!"

"She never belonged to you. Using violence with her does not give you any right to her! You are not even worthy to kiss her hands!"

Sir Frederick grabbed him angrily.

"Such a stab in the back I would never have expected from you!" he shouted. "I demand satisfaction," he added.

"I won't duel with a kin of mine."

"Fight if you are not a coward! You owe me satisfaction."

"Sometimes there is more dignity in refusing. Now I demand you to leave my house, Frederick."

Infuriated, Sir Frederick walked out.

"You and I shall not speak again. I no longer consider you a kin," he told him before leaving the house.

Jude had expected such a reaction from him, but he thought that, as much he was fond of his cousin, the loss of the fellowship of someone with such baseness of morals would not be such a great deprivation.

*[1] The "special dispensation" was a permit that allowed the fiancés to shorten the engagement time and get married sooner.

Chapter 5

One afternoon, Jude accompanied Taryn to visit his estate while they walked in the vast garden. She asked him about his family.

"Do you live here on your own?" she asked.

"My father owns some lands and properties in America. He has lived there for some years to administer the properties. I grew up with him after my mother died."

"Do you have any siblings?"

"No, I don't," he said as they stopped.

"I cannot express enough my rejoicing for you accepting me as your wife."

"I am happier than you are."

"Jude, you returned to me all I was deprived of: my respectability, the possibility of having a family. Your act proved a nobility of mind rare to find. Since then, I began to love you."

"Do you love me?" he asked, smiling. She nodded before Jude kissed her.

"You have treated me not as an object to be possessed but as a person to be honored," Taryn continued.

"Perhaps you see me better than I truly am," Jude said with

a serious look.

"Why are you saying this?"

"I too did things I am not proud of. I never attempted to any woman's honor, ever. But about three years ago, I was courting a maid of the lower class. My family wasn't content about it, my folks cared about the title, and they convinced me not to ask her in marriage."

Taryn listened carefully to Jude's tale.

"Did you love her?" she asked,

"We had barely known each other. She got married shortly after. But I regret to have been influenced by my family's view, especially my father's. He used to consider lower-class people as lesser beings. And I believe I have learned the same attitude."

"Do you think it is still so?"

"I cannot say."

"No one is perfect. We all have to improve ourselves," she said before adding "But another man if he was you would not have stood up to his own kin to help a lady who is not related to him in any way. It does you honor."

Taryn took his arm, and they walked on.

Agreed with the Pearls, Taryn and Jude set a wedding date for the earliest time possible. The Pearls received Sir Frederick's visit one day when Jude was not at home; he reproached Sir Sidney for his demotion.

"You had taken a commitment to me for Taryn's hand! Should I come to think you are a man who does not honor his own word?"

"Thee know well the circumstances of the happening had forced me to accept your request."

"Do you dare insult me after my willingness to make her an honest woman? I could have left her dishonored."

"Thee must understand if Taryn continues to refuse Your Lordship and it would become known, you know…"

"It is your fault if your daughter does not obey!" he interrupted him. "I won't tolerate such a wrong to me, the matter is not over." He walked away.

As he announced, Sir Frederick still had an "ace in a hole" to play: he took the case to the Law. In fact, the reader should know that at that time, an engagement was binding nearly as a marriage itself, and which is why Sir Frederick appealed to the commitment taken by Sir Sidney.

Sir Sidney was summoned to give a testimony. Initially, he did not know the details of the summons.

When he was before the judge, he was informed of the request made by Sir Frederick and he was questioned about the "engagement" between him and Taryn.

"Is Your Lordship aware that Thy daughter is not free to

get married with   someone else if Thee had taken a commitment with Lord Montrose before?" the judge asked him.

"Your Honor, the engagement between my daughter and the Squire Montrose had not been officialized," Sir Sidney replied.

"But is it true that Thee had committed yourself to give your daughter in marriage to Lord Montrose?"

"Your Honor, the Squire Montrose attempted to my daughter's honor. I have simply accepted the marriage as a consequence of that act."

"I should hear the two contenders confronteach other", the judge said and postponed the hearing.

Returning to the Montrose mansion, Sir Sidney informed Taryn, Mrs Pearl, and Jude of the reason for the summons. Worried, Taryn and Jude asked him about his conversation with the judge. Sir Sidney told them what he had said to the judge.

"The situation is quite complicated," commented Sir Sidney. "The judge has arranged to question me and the Squire Montrose together." Mrs Pearl asked:

"Might it be an impediment to the wedding?" Mrs Pearl asked.

"It is a concrete prospect,"Sir Sidney replied.

"I intend to give my testimony before the judge, too", Jude intervened.

Later, Jude commented on the matter with Taryn.

"If the judge declares my father's word to Sir Frederick as binding, I will not marry him," Taryn said.

"Everything will be fine, you will see," Jude tried to reassure her.

"I will be resigned to go to the monastery," Taryn said, troubled.

"Do not say that. We could have a secret wedding",

"My father says the marriage would be declared invalid."

"Have faith, Taryn. You must not give into distress, as you did not when you were forced to marry Frederick. You fought for your dignity. And it made me love you," he hugged her.

"I hardly believe I still have the strength to endure all this…", Taryn said, crying. "At least if I take the vows, I won't belong to any other man…" she said, anguished.

Taryn was grieved at the thought she might have to renounce to Jude. Sir Frederick had caused her enough humiliation, and now she had to endure more vexation because of him.

That evening, with pain in her heart, she had some time to think.

"What have I done to be the object of such harassment? Oh,

miserable life of mine! May the Lord give me the strength to endure this adversity."

When Sir Sidney was summoned again, together with Sir Frederick, Jude went along to the judge. The first to speak out was Sir Frederick.

"As I have previously declared before this, Miss Pearl and I were about to get married, with Sir Sidney Pearl's consent. My betrothed was taken away from me, in the middle of the night, by a kin of mine.."

The judge asked Sir Sidney if he could confirm Sir Frederick's words.

"I do confirm it," he replied. "Nevertheless I must specify that the agreement between me and the Squire Montrose was only made orally. no prenuptial agreement was signed."

"It does not change anything, Sir Frederick intervened. "The wedding date had been set already."

At that point, Jude asked to speak.

"Your Honor, I humbly demand to testify as Miss Pearl's current betrothed and relative of Lord Frederick Montrose." he judge agreed. "I must remark that Miss Pearl was taken by force by Lord Montrose and kept under his custody against her will," Jude said.

"We are not here to discuss about the circumstances," the judge replied.

"That led to the engagement," Jude continued. "I intended to clarify the conditions that urged Sir Sidney Pearl to accept the engagement. With his daughter dishonored he could not do otherwise.

"But later I casually made the acquaintance of Miss Pearl and I listened to her plea for help. I could not ignore her plea, so I helped her to flee from Lord Montrose's custody. And I have decided to get engaged to her not to leave her dishonored,"

"My kin had aims toward her!"Sir Frederick intervened., "Miss Pearl is de facto my wife."

"Is Your Lordship aware of this condition?" the judge addressed Jude.

"Yes, I am," he replied.

"And do you agree to marry her even in this case?" the judge asked.

"I do, Excellency, " Jude replied with complete honesty.

Sir Sidney demanded to speak.

"Your Honor, my daughter claims she would rather undertake the religious life over the marriage with the Squire Montrose," he said, "Now, I would not want to give my daughter to the monastic life. She can be quite stubborn."

"I would like to listen to the maiden," the judge affirmed. "Not she has any voice in that, but I believe it would be clarifying for the case." Then the judge dismissed them.

The reader should be aware that at that time, the Law did not grant "juridical" importance to women. They were not acknowledged as people with their own will, and they were identified by the Law in the person of the father or husband, (or any householder).

Therefore, Taryn's testimony, aside of being unusual, it had the solely purpose of providing further details about the case.

At the same moment in Montrose mansion, Taryn was conversing with her mother.

"Do you really want to take the vows?"asked Mrs. Pearl.

"I would rather do it than a life with Sir Frederick."

"You cannot imagine the relief I felt when Lord Montrose agreed to marry you."

"So did I, mother," Taryn said with teary eyes. "Do you love him?"

"Yes, mother, I love him deeply."

While they were talking, they heard Jude and Sir Sidney returning home.

The pair went to speak to them, and they asked about the audience. Sir Sidney informed Taryn about the summons. Taryn was astonished.

"Shall I speak to the judge?" she asked.

"Yes, you shall. He wants to hear your version," Sir Sidney

said. Mrs. Pearl, bewildered, intervened.

"Should she tell what happened with the Squire Montrose? It is inappropriate."

"Regrettably, we've come to this point. We cannot step back."

"What if it becomes known?" Taryn addressed to her mother. "I am not ashamed of something I am not to be blamed for."

Taryn tried to show herself confident with her family, even though she was nervous about testifying. She discussed it with Jude too, who tried to reassure her.

"What if my testimony is useless?" she asked, concerned.

"We have one more possibility: we can leave and go some other place where nobody knows us",

"Leave?",

"We can join my father in America. We could get married there. And later, we can return after some years," Jude said, holding her.

Taryn prayed intensely that night, asking for the strength to speak out before the judge with no hesitation. It was not easy for her to remember what the Squire Montrose had done to her and tell it to a stranger.

Few women or nobody before her had done such a thing. At that time, such matters were taboo, and they were scandalous, especially if heard spoken by a woman.

So, the reader can imagine Taryn's profound awkwardness and fear about doing it.

Accompanied to the judge by Jude and her father, Taryn was nervous that day, but she tried to appear confident.

The judge asked her to tell what happened the day she was taken bySir Frederick.

"I had been taken in a property of his, against my will, and kept there under the surveillance of his servants."

"Have you known Lord Frederick Montrose carnally, as he claims?" the judge asked.

Taryn was in awe of the question, but taking courage, she replied.

"I have lost consciousness, perhaps due to the dismay... so whatever happened, I have no memory of; it was not of my will."

"Did you ask Lord Jude Montrose to help Thee to flee?"

"Yes, I did."

"Lord Jude Montrose's marriage proposal, was it made before or after Thy escape?"

"After."

"Did he mention it or manifest in any way his intention before then?"

"No, Sir. Never"

"Thy father claims that Your Ladyship persists in refusing to marry Lord Frederick Montrose, and intends to undertake religious life. Is that true?"

"Yes, Excellency. It is true."

"So are you disobeying Thy family?"

"I obey my own conscience. Which prevents me from accepting to be'bought' and bestows my dignity, as all human beings. Or perhaps is it in doubt that women have soul and conscience either?"

Stunned by her answer, the judge dismissed her.

Taryn was doubtful about her testimony, if it had had the effect she had hoped. The reader might imagine the apprehension for the judge's decision during the interminable following hours. And the doubts she had in case it would have been necessary to leave Jude: should she go so far away and leave her family behind? And would her father allow her to travel with Jude?

And all this was not to oppose her fate.

☐

Chapter 6

The following day, Taryn spent most of the day in prayer and Church services, along with her mother.

There was an incident that day when a little boy, who must have beenNo more than twelve years old, he was surprised in the kitchen stealing some bread. The servants caught him, and they led him to Jude. He was about to give him some straps as a punishment, when Taryn arrived. In seeing the scene, she intervened.

"He is just a little boy."

"He was stealing in my kitchen," Jude replied.

"By his garments, I can see he must be from a poor family," she told him. "I presume the hunger drove him to steal and, as wrong as it is, the punishment seems excessive to me."

Jude was impressed by Taryn's words and he decided to let him go.

"Give him something to eat," she said.

In the afternoon was delivered the judge's summons. Taryn was taken by a perturbation, so much so that she could barely say a few words throughout the day.

The following morning, she and the Pearls went to the

judge, accompanied by Jude. They found Sir Frederick already there.

The judge spoke while everyone listened in hushed silence.

"Having heard both the parties and having known the details of the case, such as that the agreement established between Sir Sidney Pearl and Sir Frederick Montrose has been arranged only orally, I release Sir Sidney Pearl from the obligation to respect the agreement."

Taryn was deeply relieved and rejoiced, as well as Jude and the Pearls.

Sir Frederick did not take it well, but after some time, he found another lady to marry.

Taryn left her bad adventure behind either and her character was

strengthened.

In those days, Jude brought Taryn to visit the village where his subordinates lived, where they were welcomed friendly, and on that occasion, he expressed to her his intention to improve the living conditions of his laborers.

"I am also thinking about offering the sharecropping to some of them."

"I think it is a good idea."

"I am making an effort to treat these people as my equals."

"It is truly admirable of you," Taryn said, pleasantly

impressed by Jude's goodwill.

After the wedding, Taryn often visited the farmhands and their families at the borough, and she used to bring them some cakes; Taryn soon became

fondly welcomed by them.

While Taryn was carrying her first child, Lord Montrose, Jude's father, returned briefly from America to meet her.

The nobleman had a good impression of Taryn, and he was present when Taryn and Jude's son was born.

Taryn used to bring her son to the borough to play with the farmhands's kids; she taught him and her later children to treat the laborers as part of theirown family.

Taryn Pearl's case certainly was not the last one of young ladies abducted and violated for marriage purposes. But cases such as Taryn's one were precursors of the recognition of women's dignity.

Now, I leave it to the reader to make his own considerations and draw a moral from the story.

THE END

☐

Christopher

PROLOGUE

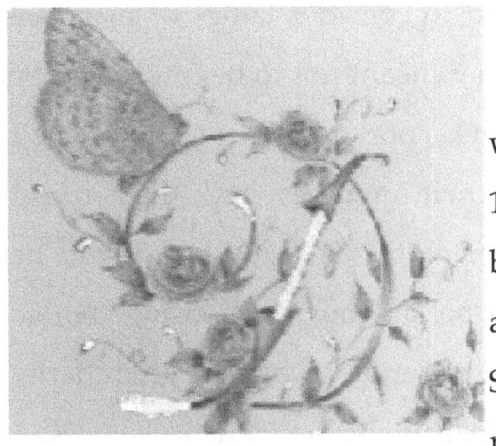

ublin, Southern Ireland.

A new Wedding Season was beginning in that year 1792 and, while the young bachelors were preparing to assist the young ladies' Society Debut, one in particular had joined them.

Christopher Wright, who did not stand out very much for his appearance, was quite ordinary, but for being one of the most serious and reliable young men, devoted to his family and religious.

All the mothers in the County would have wanted him as son-in-law. His family was one of the most known in the County, although it wasn't one of the richest, and he, as the only son, was the only heir. Being twenty-one years old by then, Christopher had decided that the time had come to choose a wife.Unlike his peers who he had a friendship with, Christopher did not overindulge in drinking and leisures, nor played at the gambling table. Moreover, he used to reproach his friends for meeting public women, considering it a "not serious" and unrestrained behavior. Christopher managed his family's business diligently, and at the same time, he never missed giving charity.

Since he and his peers had to consider ladies of marriage age to choose one, Christopher meant not to be impressed by the beauty of the Debutantes, nor by the wealth of their families, but to dwell on their qualities and their moral integrity. When he conversed with his friends about it, he used to advise them not to be shallow in choosing, but to focus on things such as: is she generous? Does she give charity to the poor ones? Is she discreet? Is she devoted?

However, not just noble women were attracted by him: on an occasion, a young lady who worked at service in his house, pushed by her mother's ambition, was determined to become his lover. One evening, she walked into his room and offered herself to him.

"How do you think I could do such a baseness?" he said before escorting her out of the room and took leave of her saying, "If I may, do not ever give up on your dignity because of your poverty. As far as I am concerned, you are noble as much as I am."

Christopher would not have imagined that soon he would be of vital importance to someone's life.

Chapter 1

It became the "spearhead" of that year's Season, the most beautiful among the Debutantes, Rochelle Chapman. Her entrance immediately dazzled all the men present. Rochelle had golden curls, big green eyes, a tall and slender figure, and white skin.

Her family did not expect less; they knew perfectly she would've caughttheir eyes, and she would've been the most courted. The Chapman family was one of the oldest in the County, but by then, they were the only ones left. Most of the Chapmans had left Ireland. The householder was Rochelle's elder brother, John, since their father had died years earlier; John was unmarried and very ambitious. He knew he had to exploit as much as he could the great fortune of having such a beautiful sister.

From the very first day after Rochelle's Debut, she began to receive so many suitors that a proper queue gathered in front of their manor. John meticulously considered the families of each one of the "candidates". Some of them were very wealthy, but he didn't want to make his choice frenzy.

About Christopher, he had seen Rochelle briefly and, although he was impressed by her beauty, he had not considered her at that moment.

However, her suitors kept on increasing, John immediately discarded those from the less wealthy families and, every time he thought he had found someone that suited her, another richest came forward.

He had considered George Williamson, whose family was very influential, and George, who was almost forty years old, was the only heir. But later, John focused his attention on more powerful families, and Williamson was quite offended because by that.

When Lady Chapman remarked with her son that it was better not to raise the bar too high, John replied.

"This is not a 'trade', and Rochelle is not a 'commodity'. She deserves the best. She could become the wife of the most powerful man in the County."

Soon, the suitors realized the pretentiousness of the Chapman family, so they began to make marriage proposals, starting a proper competition about who would make the proposal before the others. However, John, with great discomfort, declined all their proposals.

Rochelle herself was quite worried about the excessive ambition and greed of her brother, and she felt herself like a 'pawn' to use for his purposes. In the second week after her Debut, John had already dismissed most of her suitors.

Rochelle did not know anything about how the world worked. She was starting to discover it then and she was glad she could finally attend the Society events in which she was always greatly in demand for the dances.

By the end of the Season, Rochelle had received over one hundred marriage proposals; some of the men had offered her very expensive engagement rings with large and showy stones. Among her suitors, there had been counts and marquesses, but John was not satisfied with the influence of their families, and he had in mind to give her to someone that was part of the Country's politics.

Then he decided to look for some suitors outside Dublin. He had heard there were very influent families in the nearby cities, some of which were related to political men.

Rochelle's frustration became deeper day by day, and she knew that she might have to wait until the next Season to find a husband. She often confided to her mother her worries about it, even though shealways said to trust John.

"What if he chooses a husband that's too aged?" she asked, "What if he was too stingy or overbearing? Will I have to be condemned for being unhappy with a man who mistreats me or wants me just to give birth to heirs?"

Lady Chapman trusted that John knew what he was doing and that he would've made the right choice.

When John told Rochelle he was going out of town, she felt freed without the suffocating attentions of her brother, and she thought she could've taken the opportunity to visit other young ladies she had gotten to know during the Season who she was starting to confide in.

Rochelle ignored that someone moved by reprehensible intentions was lurking: Lord Williamson could not bear having been discharged by the Chapmans. Daily, he was more and more blinded by Rochelle's beauty that it obscured his gentlemanly common sense.

He had placed two servants on guard in front of Chapman mansion, and they had watched John leaving. Later, Rochelle went to visit the ladies nearly every day.

Rochelle was usually accompanied by her mother, but later she allowed her to go alone with her personal maid. During one of these visits while traveling on a country road, Rochelle's carriage was approached by Lord Williamson's servants, who forced them to stop.

They pulled Rochelle and her maid down, and they ordered Rochelle to go along with them to visit their master. Frightened Rochelle asked them who their master was and why he hadn't come himself. The servants grabbed her badly and tried to drag her away, so Rochelle cried out. The maid also cried out for helpIt just so happened that Christopher was riding nearby.

Hearing the cry, Christopher intervened and ordered the two men to leave. They tried to intimidate him, but Christopher spoke to them.

"I know who you are, and I know who your master is. If you don't leave, I'll charge you to the constables."

The pair then gave up.

"We apologize. We've made a mistake. We mistook the young lady for another person. Forgive the disturbance." With that said, they left.

Rochelle was shocked and nearly fainted, her coachman laid her down inside the carriage.:

"My home is nearby," Christoper said. "It is better to take her there and send for the doctor".

So the carriage followed Christopher to Wright mansion. Once there, Christopher instructed the servants to bring Rochelle in one of the chambers and he sent for the doctor.

Rochelle got better pretty quick while she was assisted by her maid. Christopher offered to send for her householder, but the maid informed him that he was out of town.

Rochelle was visited by the doctor, who gave her water with sugar and said it was just a passing indisposition due to the fright. Indeed, Rochelle was better shortly afterward and she wanted to get up, asking to speak to Christopher.

During their conversation Christopher introduced himself.

"I wanted to thank you for your intervention and for your assistance," Rochelle told him.

"You can stay here all the time necessary for you to recover," Christopher said. "So you are Miss Chapman?"

"Ay, Rochelle Chapman," she replied.

"I recognized those men. They were servants of Lord George Williamson." Rochelle was astonished to hear that. "Does your family have any quarrel with Lord Williamson?"

"No. Except that Lord Williamson was one of my suitors," she replied.

Christopher's face held a look of suspicion.

"Now I understand," he said.

"I was informed by your maid that Mr. Chapman is out of town," she replied. "He is, indeed. My brother has been gone for three days, and I presume he will be gone for a few days more,"

"I am feeling better now," she continued." The doctor said it was a passing indisposition. I believe I can leave."

"I believe it is not safe for you to go alone," he replied. "I will escort you."

Rochelle thanked him.

"Now that your brother is out of town Lord Williamson might try to have you kidnapped again," he informed her.

"Do you believe that?" she asked him, looking at him with worry.

"I know Lord Williamson enough and he is not a man to be intimidated so easily," Christopher replied." Sadly, some men use this kind of means."

"Why would he do that?" she asked in confusion.

"To force you to marry him," he replied. Vexed, Rochelle was speechless. "I believe those 'methods' are reprehensible, but some men find them acceptable."

Rochelle was frightened and confused by that situation, but Christopher consoled her.

"Maybe I should speak to your mother and ask her to allow you to stay here until your brother is returned."

"Staying here?" she asked in surprise.

"Here you will have protection," he assured her.

"I do not want to cause any disturbance. You have already done enough for me."

"I insist," he told her with a comforting smile. "Of course, you'll have your coziness. This evening you can meet my mother."

"Thank you for your kindness," she replied.

Christopher immediately sent for Lady Chapman, who was led there. Meanwhile, the Wrights returned home, and Christopher introduced Rochelle to them.

"I knew your father. A great man," Mr Wright informed her.

"Sadly, I cannot remember much of him,"Rochelle replied.

"Miss Chapman will be our guest for a few days," Christopher told his parents.

"In this case, we'll have time to get to know each other,".Lady Wright commented.

When Lady Chapman arrived, Christopher and the Wrights informed her about what had happened, and she was shocked to learn of the attempted kidnapping, and she agreed that it was safer for Rochelle to stay there until John's return.

"I cannot believe Lord Williamson has been capable of such a despicable act!" she exclaimed. "I don't dare to imagine could have happened to her!"

"Sadly some men use to do that," Christopher remarked.

"I really don't know how to thank you enough for your assistance to my daughter and for the support you are offering to her, Sir Christopher," Lady Chapman replied. "May the Lord bless you".

Christopher arranged for Rochelle to have a private maid assigned, but she declined since she had already the assistance of her personal maid. That evening, she dined with the Wrights, who offered to show her their manor the following day.

"Do you ride?" asked Mr. Wright.

"Actually, I cannot do it very well," she replied.

"We could take her with the calash", Christopher suggested.

That evening, Christopher as usual trained with boxing until the nightfall before taking a cold bath, with the addition of a little bit of ice, and went to sleep. In the morning, he awoke pretty early and, after taking another freeze bath, he went to the house's Chapel to say the morning prayers.

So he was ready to face another day.

☐

Chapter 2

That day, Christopher and his mother accompanied Rochelle to see the manor with the calash. Their property was not very vast, but included a beautiful countryside surrounded by big trees. They spent the whole morning visiting it and conversing. Rochelle conversed mostly with Lady Wright, and she was pleasantly impressed by Rochelle.

When they returned home, Lady Wright spoke briefly with Christopher.

"Miss Chapman is a very kind and refined lady."

"I agree," Christopher replied.

"As far as I know she is not betrothed to anyone yet," she continued."She might be good as a wife for you."

"Lady Chapman said her brother went out of town to find her an husband,"he responded "I suppose he will return with a betrothed for her. Besides, about the unpleasant event that occurred with Lord Williamson early this morning, I have met my friend Paul and confided to him what happened. He told me some rumors circulating about Lord Williamson."

"What kind of rumors?" Lady Wright asked.

"They say he already has a wife," Christopher replied. "They said he married a woman of a lower family a few months ago, and he abandoned her just after the wedding."

"I cannot believe what you're saying!" Lady Wright explaimed in bewilderment.

"That man is even worse than I thought," Christopher commented "He has no decency!".

Indeed, Lord Williamson had no intention of giving up on his purpose, andsomehow, he had found out that Rochelle was hosted at Wright mansion. Attempting another kidnapping in those circumstances was too risky, so he thought about sending something else to deliver a letter to Rochelle at Wright mansion.

In the late afternoon, Rochelle received the letter.

"Respectable Miss Chapman, the humble Undersigned dares to write to Thee, despite not having the right to do it, to ask You to forgive my reckless behavior.

I have forgotten the manners of a gentleman to make a shameful act, of which I have now understood the graveness.

Your brother's refusal to my proposal had enraged me to the point of pushing me to think of illicit means to have You as a wife. I had thought You would have had the opportunity to get to know me, and then You would have agreed to become my spouse. I ask for your forgiveness for the damage I have caused to Thee. I have disrespected You and my own good Name.

If You would allow me to be received by Your Ladyship in Wright mansion to personally ask for your forgiveness, I shall be grateful and I would repair my honor, as well as Your own.

Your Servant,

Lord G. Williamson".

Rochelle was perplexed by that letter, and in the evening, she decided to confide that to Lady Wright and Christopher.

Christopher was suspicious and advised Rochelle not to receive Lord Williamson.

"That man cannot be trusted," he said.

"If he intends simply to ask for forgiveness, should I deny it?" Rochelle observed and then continued."However it is not necessary for me to receive him here.I do not want to embarrass you in any way. And you have already done enough for me. I think he would be agreed to wait for me to return to Chapman mansion."

"If you are willing to receive Lord Williamson I will not certainly prevent it," Christopher replied. "However here, with our surveillance, nothing can happen to you."

"Thank you, Sir Christopher," Rochelle responded.

"Speaking of each, there is something I think you should know," he continued. "I have heard rumors about Lord Williamson being an extremely unreliable man. I usually do not pay attention to gossip, but the rumors seem trustworthy to me."

"Is there something in particular you are referring to?" she asked.

"They say Lord Williamson has already a wife," he informed her.

Rochelle was bewildered, but Christopher continued.

"In my opinion, a man who does not respect his own wife is unable to respect any woman. However, if he truly repents his behavior and he wishes to ask for forgiveness, it would be unfair to deny him the opportunity."

Rochelle agreed with Christopher, and then she retired.

The following day, Rochelle sent someone to deliver her response to Lord Williamson, and the same day, he went to Wright mansion. He was received by Christopher and Rochelle. Christopher stood there all the time.

"First of all, I wish to apologize to Thee, Sir Christopher, for the inconvenience caused by my servants," Lord Williamson spoke first.

Christopher replied with just a nod, and Lord Williamson then spoke to Rochelle

"I know what I have done has no justifications. I have dishonored Thee and myself, and I beg your pardon."

"I accept Thy apologies, Lord Williamson,"Rochelled replied

"I am grateful," he responded. "I was seriously willing to take you as a wife if your brother had not declined my proposal. And, if you are not betrothed to someone else, I intend to repair the dishonor by renewing my proposal to him."

"I am certain there is nothing to repair, Rochelle said in shock. "And it is not necessary for my brother to be informed about the event that occurred. I shall speak to my mother, and I'll ask her for discretion as well."

"I am grateful for this," Lord Williamson said and then took leave. Christopher walked him outside.

As they were walking to Lord Williamson's carriage, he spoke to Christopher.

"If you are thinking of courting Miss Chapman, be aware she is not for someone like you."

"Everything regarding miss Chapman is no longer of Your Lordship's concern," Christopher replied in annoyance.

"You are not wealthy enough for her brother's standards," Lord Williamson replied. "I can offer her a privileged position."

"What about Thy legitimate wife?" Christopher asked. "Everyone in the neighborhood is aware of that."

"You should be concerned about finding a wife for yourself, Wright, he quickly said in surprise. "Or maybe a lover, as everyone does. And leave Miss Chapman alone."

"Does Your Lordship think my family would want me to waste our money to keep women? Christopher replied."This is not what I was taught."

"Do as you please, but stay away from miss Chapman," Lord Williamson stated before he got in the carriage and left.

Later, Christopher discussed the conversation with Mr. and Mrs. Wright.

"That man is ambiguous, and I believe he still represents a threat," Christopher said.

"John Chapman should be informed about that when he will be returned," his father suggested.

"I agree," Christopher said. "I am indignant by some people's shallowness. You, father, have taught me to respect women and to treat them as my equals, and I am grateful to you for your teachings."

"During these twenty-one years, you've never given us any reason for disappointment," Mr Wright commented.

"You don't have to say that," Christopher replied. "I will never dishonor my family and my reputation with excesses as some men do."

During the Season that just ended, Christopher met several Debutantes and, although some of them had good qualities, Christopher found their temperament quite passive. When he asked questions about their opinions, they provided generic phrases, expressing only what a suitor would want to hear.They seemed to have none of their own opinions about some matters. Instead, they used those tailored to family members and suitors.

Christopher understood that sadly they had been educated to behave like that, and by then, he was losing hope of finding a suitable companion

As Christopher had suspected about Lord Williamson, he was not defeated at all, and the following day, Rochelle received a visit from his servant who delivered her a missive from the Nobleman. In the letter, Lord Williamson tried to explain the matter of his previous marriage and why he had not mentioned it to Rochelle:

"Respectable Miss Chapman, my letter is motivated by my sense of duty to give You explanations regarding a question that damages my reputation and disrespects Your own.

I have been informed that You are aware of my previous marriage with a lady, whom, for discretion, I do not mention the name. It is true; I had contracted a marriage, of which there was no consummation. My wife and I decided after a brief time to ask the Church for an annulment. Therefore, I have decided to consider another wife so I can remarry as soon as it is possible.

I have avoided mentioning this matter so as not to compromise the judgment of the families regarding my reliability. I assure You that I never intended to lie or deceive You, or your family.

I will be available soon, and I will be able to provide for You and your family, if Mr. Chapman would accept me as a brother-in-law. I apologize to Thee, and I remain,

Your humble Servant,

Lord G. Williamson".

Rochelle felt obliged to reply to the letter and to clarify the question with Lord Williamson.

"Most Respectable Lord Williamson, I understood by reading Your Lordship's letter Thy reasons, and I refrain myself from expressing judgments on Thy decisions.

However, I must inform Thee that a possible engagement between us is barred not only by Thy previous marriage but also by my family's disapproval and other matters.

The humble Undersigned is certain that Your Lordship shall find a betrothed more worthy than I am, and I wish Thee a prosperous life and a joyful marriage.

Greeting in friendship, Thy humble Servant,

Rochelle Chapman."

In the afternoon, Rochelle mentioned Lord Williamson's letter to Lady Wright, and she expressed her suspicions about

Lord Williamson.

"Be careful with men acting like that," she told her. "They try to take advantage of inexperienced young ladies as you are, who don't know how the world goes."

Christopher casually listened to part of their conversation and he misunderstood the emphasis Rochelle used, even though he acted as nothing had happened in presence of her.

That evening while meeting Rochelle catching air in the garden, he talked to her briefly. He could not hold back some phrases of disappointment.

"I thought I had done you a favor by welcoming you in my house and keeping you away from Lord Williamson."

"Of course you did."

"Is it so? I have heard that you continue to correspond with Lord Williamson."

"He just sent me a letter to clarify the question of his previous marriage, and I felt obliged to reply, bewildered by his words."

"Do you have feelings for Lord Williamson?"

"Of course I don't," she replied, stunned "I simply wanted to make it clear I do not have any resentment for him."

"Men like him know how to attract women. They use power, luxury, promises…"

"I don't understand what your point is, Sir Christopher. Do

you think I am so naive?" Rochelle was very annoyed by Christopher's tone.

"I apologize. This does not concern me," he said and took his leave.

That night, he trained more than usual in boxing, trying to push away that strange sense of nuisance he felt over his body. The following morning, Rochelle went to the Church with the Wrights, and then she received a visit from Lady Chapman. She avoided mentioning Lord Williamson's letter; she did not want her mother to be concerned about nothing.

That afternoon, however, Rochelle received another visit from Lord Williamson's servant, who gave her a new letter.

"Respectable Miss Chapman; I know I have no right to address Thee again; I trust that You will consider what I have to say to You.

I know your brother is looking for another betrothed for You. However, I intend to show my generosity towards Thee and Thy family by registering one of my properties out of Dublin in your family's Name. I also own several properties in Ireland, and your brother can choose among them the one that pleases him the most.

As members of my own family, your kins shall have all my possessions as they please as their disposal.

This, I hope, would show my seriousness and reliability in

Your Ladyship's eyes, and your family's.

Thy humble Servant,

Lord G. Williamson."

Rochelle was impressed by Lord Williamson's proposal, and she thought she should inform her mother about it so that she could make the right decision after consulting John. But in the end, she decided to reply to Lord Williamson herself.

"Most Respectable Lord Williamson, I thank Your Lordship for the generous proposal and for the kindness shown to me.

However, I must remind Your Grace that my brother decides which man I will marry, not me. When he returns, Your Grace can ask him for an audience and propose to him Thy offers for Yourself.

Furthermore, I humbly ask Your Lordship to remember that Thy previous marriage has not been declared null by the Church at the moment, and there is no guarantee that Thy request will be accepted.

Thanking Your Grace for Thy patience,

I give my Best Regards.

Thy humble Servant,

Rochelle Chapman".

Lord Williamson did not take long to reply to the letter, making a proposal that left Rochelle perplexed.

"Respectable Miss Chapman, I thank You for your previous

reply, and regarding your doubts about the annulment of my previous marriage, I would like to remark that my engagement with You does not necessarily have to be legally valid. My own word is enough to guarantee the respectable life You deserve. We could hold a symbolic ceremony and maintain discretion with the society, so in their eyes, we would be married.

My commitment to You will be sanctioned by my word. You will own my Name and my Title. I intend to speak to your brother as soon as he returns.

With all my esteem,

Your humble Servant,

Lord G. Williamson".

Rochelle could not believe that Lord Williamson had made such a proposal.She felt outraged. That same day, she had her reply delivered to Lord Williamson.

"Most Respectable Lord Williamson, Thy last letter was the cause of great disappointment for me. I am offended in my honor by the proposal that Your Lordship made. Does Your Grace think I would lower myself to live together with a man who is another woman's husband? And does Your Grace believe my family would accept it?

If Thy annulment request is accepted, only then can we discuss the question again. Trusting that Your Lordship will understand my reasons,

I give my Best Regards.

Your humble Servant,

Rochelle Chapman".

Rochelle was so annoyed that she wanted to confide in Lady Wright.Rochelle was even ashamed to talk about such a proposal.

"I am astonished as much you are, my dear," she told her. "But, I must admit that it doesn't surprise me very much. He is neither the first nor the last to make such proposals."

In that moment Christopher walked in.

"What kind of proposal are you talking about?" he asked, but Lady Wright diverted his attention.

"Nothing particular. We are discussing one of Miss Chapman's first suitors." They began to talk about something else, but soon Rochelle preferred to retire.

When she was gone, Christopher spoke to his mother.

"You were talking about Lord Williamson earlier, weren't you? I am not stupid."

"We were," Lady Wright replied. "But, I did not want Miss Chapman to be embarrassed."

"I see," Christopher said. "And what kind of proposal were you talking about?"

"Well, you know, he cannot be certain his marriage will be

declared null…" she started replying.

Christopher figured out what his mother was trying to say and interrupted her.

"Tell me he did not ask her what I am thinking," he said. Lady Wright did not answer, and her silence was enough confirmation for Christopher.

Indignant, Christopher got up and walked away in a rush, ignoring his mother's questions. Lady Wright was concerned about Christopher's reaction, but for the moment, she preferred to wait and not mention it to anyone.

Chapter 3

That evening, Christopher went to Williamson's park and asked to be received by Lord Williamson. When he arrived, Christopher greeted him.

"Forgive me for the time, but I needed to speak to Your Lordship urgently," he told him.

"I believe I have nothing to discuss with Thee, Sir Christopher," claimed Lord Williamson.

"I am here because of a matter that I deeply care about," Christopher said. "I truly care about Miss Chapman, and above all things, I would never bear to see something unfortunate happening to her."

"You have no reason to be worried about that," Lord Williamson replied.

"I am aware of the proposal Thee have made," Christopher said.

"With all due respect, Thee are not her tutor," Lord Williamson replied.

"This is true, but Miss Chapman is momentarily under my protection," Christopher replied.

"It is only a matter of time. before Mr. Chapman returns, and I shall discuss the matter with him."

"Do you want to humiliate your good name further? And disrespect Miss Chapman's name and her family's? Do you really believe a respectable family could ever accept such a condition?"

"I know her brother's ambition; men like him would give anything for a prominent position."

"Mr. Chapman has already declined your proposal once. And by now, he must have found a betrothed for Miss Chapman."

"Or perhaps you would like to be that betrothed, would you not?"

"I don't have such an illusion. I am here just because your proposal has insulted Miss Chapman. A man who offends a lady also offends himself. Therefore, if Your Grace owns a sense of honor, please, desist from "

Lord Williamson took some whiskey and paused for a while.

"You know, you speak as if you know women. But, according with what I have heard, you don't. You cannot know if Miss Chapman is tempted to accept my proposal."

"I know good manners. And I believe it is reprehensible that our Society accepts kidnapping and depriving women of their honor as means to force them to marriage."

"This is how the world has always worked; I did not invent

any of this."

"It does not matter. We must obey the precepts of morality and decency. I hope you'll understand that."

Then Christopher took his leave and left the manor. But he knew very well that his words had annoyed Lord Williamson more than ever, and he had taken them as defiance.

The following day, Christopher was planning to speak to Rochelle about that, but he had not had the chance since she received her mother's visit.

Lady Chapman informed her that she had received news from John.

"John wrote me telling he has met a lady and he intends to court her," Lady Chapman said, "which is why he is going to stay there for some time." She also said that she had already informed Lady Wright about it.

"I did not mean to be a burden for the Wrights further," Rochelle said. "Perhaps I should return home."

"Lady Wright suggests that you should stay," her mother replied. "About an eventual betrothed for you, John did not mention anything about it. Perhaps he has not found someone suitable yet."

Rochelle did not mention to her mother about Lord Williamson's proposal. However, she later learned from Lady Wright about Christopher's visit to Lord Williamso.

"Was it because of me that Sir Christopher has argued with Lord Williamson?" Rochelle asked in astonishment.

"I presume it was for defending your honor," Lady Write replied. "But he did not want to tell further."

Concerned, Rochelle sought Christopher, and she found him on the balcony.

"I was looking for you, Sir," she told him.

"Tell me, Miss Chapman," he replied.

"Your mother informed me about your visit to Lord Williamson last night."

"I went to visit Lord Williamson, it is true. I wanted to talk to him man to man."

"It wasn't necessary for you to do that. You've already done enough for me."

"I just tried to remind Lord Williamson of his own honor."

"I do not want any quarrels between you and Lord Williamson."

"Are you worried for me or for him?" Christopher asked her, taunted by her doubts.

"I don't know what you mean."

"I have been informed that you continue to correspond with Lord Williamson."

"Answering letters is education," she replied in embarrasment.

"Did you ever give him any reason to hope?"

"I did not, obviously."

"Are you sure?"

"You are offending me, Sir Christopher," Rochelle replied, disappointed by his words.

"Forgive me, I don't have a temper strong enough to endure all this," he said, taking his leave.

"What did he mean with those words?" Rochelle wondered, having not understood his last phrase.

During dinner, Christopher said no words to Rochelle, and he did not even look at her. Rochelle did not understand his attitude, and she seriously thought about leaving that house.

In the afternoon, she received a letter from Lord Williamson.

"Respectable Miss Chapman, I would like to apologize to Thee for unintentionally offending you with my previous letter. It wasn't my intention to disrespect You.

You have my word that I will do everything in my power to obtain the annulment of my marriage, for I wish above all things that Thee would be my wife.

To prove my dedication to Thee, I have demanded my servant to give You the engagement ring I have chosen as my marriage proposal to Thee. I also would like to register my Palace downtown on your name, of which You can dispose of as Thee and your family please.

I hope that all this is enough to make You understand my regret for offending You and my solemn pledge to take Thee as a wife.

Thy humble Servant,

Lord G. Williamson".

Rochelle was astonished by his words, but she did not want to accept the ring, and she didn't even open the box. Instead, she delivered her response in a letter to him via his servant

"Most Respectable Lord Williamson, I accept Thy apologies, and I thank Your Lordship for the ring and for the rest, but conventions demand me to decline. I cannot accept anything from Your Grace before my has accepted Thy proposal and given his consent.

I trust Your Lordship would understand and would have the patience to wait for my brother's return.

I thank Your Grace,

Thy humble Servant,

Rochelle Chapman".

Lord Williamson's answer did not take long to arrive:

"Respectable Miss Chapman, I understand perfectly your reticence in accepting my generosity, and I understand your willingness to respect conventions and to wait for your brother's consent.

However, I would like to remark that these days, it is not unusual for some couples in England to formalize the marriage, not being obliged to submit to the will of families.

I also would like, once we have formalized our union, to take Thee with me on a journey to Europe. We could stay away even for a year and visit Paris, Berlin, Venice, etc., and maybe even go to America.

As Lady Williamson, You will have a personal maid and three servants. I won't mind the expenses, and You will be treated as You deserve. I will not deny anything to You.

Waiting for your reply,

I give You my Best Regards.

Thy humble Servant,

Lord G. Williamson".

Rochelle was upset more than ever by Lord Williamson's words, and she did not know how to formulate an answer without offending him, so she decided not to reply for the moment.

However, due to Christopher's distrust of her, she decided to leave Wright mansion. When she told explained what had happened to Lady Wright, she was saddened and insisted that Rochelle stay with her because she was safer there. However, Rochelle was convinced about her decision.

"Your Ladyship has treated me as a member of your own

family, and I would never be grateful enough," Rochelle said. "If Your Grace allows me, I would like to visit this house sometimes."

"Of course you can. I would be glad," Lady Wright told her.

Christopher was not in the house that evening since he had gone to meet some friends. Lady Wright said she would inform him about her decision the following morning.

Chapter 4

When Christopher returned that evening, he noticed that after the last conversations with Rochelle, he was feeling more restless than usually when he went to bed. So, during the evening cold bath, he tried to distract his mind by focusing on something else.

The following morning, he went to confession and opened his heart completely,

"It is normal to desire a woman," the Confessor told him.

"That woman is not for me," Christopher said, doubtful.

Since he had been delayed by the confession, Christopher missed Rochelle's departure, and he was informed shortly after. Confused, he asked for explanations from his mother.

"Didn't we decide it was safer for her to stay here until her brother's return?" he asked. "How long is she been gone?"

"A few minutes," a servant replied.

Christopher rushy walked out, took his horse, and then he ran after Rochelle's carriage.

He found it halfway and approached it. Rochelle, surprised to see Christopher, got off the carriage.

"What are you doing here?" she asked.

"You could have   informed me about your decision to

leave, milady," Christopher said.

"Your mother told me she would inform you," Rochelle replied. Christopher got down the horse.

"Is it because of me that you have made this decision?" he asked.

"I have decided that it's because you and your family have already done more than necessary for me, Sir Christopher."

"Lord Williamson still represents a threat to you."

"I believe Lord Williamson has understood his mistakes."

"Do you believe? You don't know men, Miss Chapman."

"It is not for you to protect me, Sir Christopher."

"Do you want to be protected? Or are you considering marrying Lord Williamson?"

"Please! You know very well he is not available at the moment. You've already outraged me enough with your allusions, Sir," Rochelle said, upset.

"Forgive me. It wasn't my intention to offend you."

"You have a poor opinion of me, don't you?" she asked him.

"What makes you think that?"

"What is that bothers you so much, Sir Christopher?"

"Greed," he finally replied after a momet's hesitation. "It is something I cannot stand. I have never exceeded in my ambition."

"Are you referring to my brother?"she asked, bewildered.

"I do not intend to offend your folks."

"You think I am the same as him, don't you?" Rochelle asked with heart in tumult.

Christopher did not answer, and she opened the carriage door to get in, but Christopher stopped her.

"Please, wait."

"You think I am shallow, don't you?" Rochelle asked in utter disapoointment. "Have you ever thought to ask me directly?"

"I have no right to ask," he said in an annoyed tone.

"But you made a judgment on my character so hastily!"

"You are right; I have been arrogant," Christopher said, perplexed."But now, please, go back."

"You do not owe me anything. I deliver you from any duty towards me," Rochelle said, getting into the carriage.

"Please allow me to make amends. I could never forgive myself if something happened to you."

Rochelle did not answer, so Christopher addressed the coachman:

"To Wright mansion."

The carriage went back. Rochelle was confused. Christopher had some shades that she could not understand.

When they returned to Wright mansion, Lady Wright was

surprised and glad to see Rochelle again. Christopher demanded a room be prepared for her, and she decided not to dine that night.She retired to her room.

Christopher stayed to converse with Lady Wright, taken by doubts about his behavior with Rochelle.

"I think I have formed a wrong opinion about Miss Chapman," he said.

"What you mean?" Lady Wright asked.

"This situation with Lord Williamson has altered my judgment," he replied. "Do you think that I am superb?"

"Why on earth do you believe you are superb?"asked Lady Wright.

"I have always tried to follow the precepts of morality. I have always hated lust and materialism," Christopher said, "which is why I do not consider the wealth of the Debutantes's families. I could even marry a woman of a lower class, if she would possess the qualities that really matter."

"And Miss Chapman, doesn't she posses them?"Lady Wright asked him.

"I don't know what to think about her," Christopher asked despondently. "And besides, I cannot aspire to be accepted by the Chapmans. You know perfectly that I have never dedicated myself to improving our status. I have never made any investments or tried to increase our patrimony."

"And me and your father have always supported this attitude of yours," Lady Wright replied.

"Why should I join a family thatonly sees my position?" Christopher asked.

"It is she that you have to accept, not her family,"Lady Wright replied. "Families are important, but her attributes are all that matter.

"This is the problem," he said. "Today Miss Chapman made me understand that I have judged her too hastily, and I have been superb."

"Everyone makes mistakes," she informed him. "Don't be so strict with yourself."

Christopher did not answer and tried to think about his mother's words.

That evening, he had been thinking so long about his conversation with Rochelle.He struggled to fall asleep; he got up and went to perform his boxing training until late night.

☐

Chapter 5

Rochelle also had the opportunity to think about both the conversation with Christopher and the situation with Lord Williamson. That morning, she decided to make it clear regarding the question with Lord Williamson and sent him a reply letter.

"Most Respectable Lord Williamson, with all due respect, I am obliged to remark to Your Grace that the only answer I could ever give to Thy offer could not certainly be positive. Does Your Lordship believe I could ever be such a disappointment to my family? And that I would lose my respectability by taking such a risk and shame my family?

Does Your Lordship believe that my family would accept richnesses and properties provided by their relative's perdition?

If Your Grace has so great consideration for me that wants me as a wife, do not offend me by making such a proposal as that. My dignity and my conscience cannot be bought with material goods.

I have forgiven Your Lordship for the reckless act Thee have made in my regards, but I will not tolerate any more impudence by Your Lordship. Your Grace, and I will not be discussing the matter again until my brother has returned.

Trusting that Your Lordship understands my reasons,

I give my Best Regards.

Thy humble Servant,

Rochelle Chapman".

Of course, Lord Williamson did not take the answer well, as it hurt his pride. He was a cunning man and made up trickery to carry out his original plan.It was not difficult for him to find a servant in Wright mansion who, in return for some silver, would've been available to do as he asked.

The best time to carry it out was in the evening, after dinner time, when most of the servants had already retired. In that hour, Rochelle used to retire in the Chapel to say her prayers; the servant would have let

Lord Williamson's henchmen got in through one of the back doors. Once Rochelle had been taken, they would've put on her a coat with a maid headset to disguise her.

Unbeknown to this, Christopher that evening discussed with his father about Rochelle and about his doubts.

"Miss Chapman and her family are not the same thing," Mr. Wright said.

"It is not sure that Miss Chapman shares her brother's ambition and greed," Christopher replied.

"And yet she is still corresponding with Lord Williamson,"

Mr. Wright observed.

"That man never ceases to reserve unpleasant surprises…" Christopher said. "A man who wants a woman under such conditions as kidnapping is not worthy to have one. Besides, what sort of man is someone who marries a woman and abandons her shortly afterward? Would it be worthyof the word of someone who doesn't keep his commitments?"

"However, you cannot blame Miss Chapman for simply replying to his letters," Mr Wright told him. "I understand your wish to find a spouse who shares the integrity you have chosen for yourself. But you don't have to be so strict."

"That is what I was reflecting on; I have exceeded in it superbly," Chrsistopher commented. "And I did it in a shallow way. Miss Chapman is right to feel belittled because of this."

"I am certain you will know how to make amends," Mr Wright replied..

Christopher intended to talk to Rochelle, but then he thought waiting until the following morning was better.

Rochelle went to the Chapel and knelt on the prie-dieu when suddenly a man showed up from behind the altar: Rochelle leaped, but she thought he was one of the servants.

"I did not know someone was here," the man said nothing and approached her. She stood up suspiciously,

"Who are you?" she asked, and she heard the door opening behind her; she turned, but the man grabbed her and put a hand on her mouth. Rochelle wriggled, frightened, and the other man, as soon as he walked in, held her arms.

The pair lifted her and carried her outside, where the corrupted servant was waiting, but Rochelle managed to bite the henchman's hand, and she cried out.

Christopher had heard the cry, who ran there and caught them as they were trying to get out of a back door.

"Let her go!" he shouted, one of them showed a knife and threatened him.

"Let us leave," the man also showed a pistol in the belt, but Christopher wasn't frightened at all.

"You won't get far. I'll send my servants after you as soon as you get through that door!"

The other man dragged Rochelle through the door.

"What if we harm the lady?" he asked.

"So you'll be accused of harming a noblewoman as well?" Christopher asked in reply."Let her go, and I'll let you leave."

Reluctantly, the pair at last left Rochelle go and fled. Christopher rushed to her and took her in his arms.

"Are you hurt?" she fainted, and Christopherlifted her up.

He brought her to her room, where her maid was waiting, and he laid her on the bed. She was conscious, and she didn't want the doctor to be called.

The Wrights were informed about what had happened, and they rushed to ask about her.

"They were Lord Williamson's men," Christopher said.

"Even in our own home?!" exclaimed Mr. Wright.

"I'll tell the servants to patrol the house, especially in the night," Christopher said.

Christopher first questioned the traitorous servant, but he claimed that the pair had threatened him with the knife and forced him to let them in. Christopher was not convinced by the tale, and it seemed strange to him that the pair had risked breaking in the house.Moreover, the pair must have known that Rochelle was in the Chapel. Christopher then decided to dismiss the servant.

Then Christopher took his horse and rode to Williamson park.

He asked for Lord Williamson, but he was denied seeing the Noble. Furious, he got on the horse and shouted.

"Lord Williamson, I challenge you to a duel tomorrow at dawn! We will fight with pistols. If you are a man of honor, show up tomorrow!" He repeated that a second time and then he rode away. Lord Williamson had heard that from his house, and he had no intention of stepping back.

Convinced that the had more experience than Christopher

in the use of weapons, Lord Williamson was certain he would beat him.

The Wrights, when they learned about the duel, tried to convince Christopher to desist.

"You're not used to using weapons," Mr. Wright said.

"And I believed you were against the use of weapons," Christopher replied. "Do you think I want to kill him? It is not a last-blood duel."

"Even so, it is not a guarantee that Williamson will not kill you," Mr Wright told him.

"It is a risk I must take," Christopher said. "His men have broken into my own house. It is a defiance I cannot tolerate."

"Have you not thought about us?" Lady Wright asked. "What if something happens to you?!"

"If I don't fight him, how could we be sure he won't do it again?" Christopher replied. "What sort of man would I be if I couldn't defend my own home?".

Lady Wright had heartache thinking of what Lord Williamson was capable of; that evening, she confided it to Rochelle, informing her about the duel. Rochelle was vexed to learn that Christopher had challenged Lord Williamson.

"It is because of me this is happening!" she said with teary eyes. "I have only caused trouble to your family!"

"I do not blame you for any of this," Lady Wright reassured

her. "You are just a victim of that man."

"I should not have stayed here," Rochelle continued, regardless of her words. Before Lady Wright could say anything else, she took her leave and went to find Christopher.

He had spent all the evening in the countryside training in shooting and improving his aim. When he returned home, Rochelle went to meet him.

"I was told about the duel. Please, you don't have to do it; do not risk your life because of me,"

"That is not the only reason I wan to do it," Christopher replied. "Lord Williamson sent his men to break into my house. I must defend my honor too, not just yours."

"It would not have happened if I had not been here. You should have let me go,"

"Do not feel guilty...," Christopher said resignedly.

"I intend to remedy the situation," Rochelle replied. "I 'll let Lord Williamson know that I shall consider his proposal. In return, I shall ask him not to accept the duel."

"You cannot do such a thing," Christopher said in astonishment.. "You cannot throw your life away!"

"And neither can you with your own!" Rochelle replied.

"I will not let you do this, even if I have to keep you in your room locked!" Christopher stepped into the corridor door and called a servant: "Escort Miss Chapman to her room and stay before the door. Make sure she won't get out and she won't send any correspondence to anyone."

Hearing those word,s Rochelle was anguished.

All through the night, she could not sleep, and she prayed a long time for nothing to happen to Christopher.

In the morning, the Wrights insisted on accompanying him, and, learning about that, Rochelle asked permission to go along.

Christopher was already there, and by the time they arrived, he and Lord Williamson were about to choose their weapons.

Then they flipped the coin to determine who wouldshoot first first;it fell to Lord Williamson.

With the heart beating, Rochelle watched them take up positions; Lord Williamson aimed for Christopher's chest, and Christopher held his breath.One gunshot, and a gush of blood slipped from Christopher's neck. Rochelle leaped, but Christopher was still standing. The wound on the side of his neck was just a smear.

The doctor approached him, while the man who presided over the duel asked Lord Williamson if he was satisfied.

"I am not," he replied, knowing he was taking a risk. He could have stopped the duel then and kept his honor as a winner, but injuring Christopher was not enough for him. He wanted to make him pay for ruining his plans twice.

Christopher signed to the doctor to let him know he did not need him and took up the position again. Since Christopher had no intention of foul play, he aimed for Lord Williamson's arm;the bullet shot him just below the elbow, superficially.

Christopher raised his hand holding the gun and spoke.

"I am satisfied."

"I am not satisfied yet!" Lord Williamson shouted.

"The terms were clear, Sir. It is not a last-blood duel. So we are even."

Rochelle and the Wrights were relieved, while Christopher went to have his wound medicated.

Lord Williamson approached the Wright's carriage carrying a pack of papers.

"These are yours, I return them to you!" he said to Rochelle furiously and threw the papers to the ground.Rochelle figured out that those were her letters, but she did not want to pick them up and left them there.

Christopher had seen that scene, and Lord Williamson addressed him next.

"That woman is yours now; you can take her!" He turned his back walking away.

Once the Wright's carriage was gone, Christopher,

suspicious, went to pick up the letters.

Returned to Wright mansion, Rochelle and Lady Wright conversed briefly. Rochelle was still feeling guilty about what had happened.

"Don't think about it anymore, my child," Lady Wright told her."I never thought you were to blame."

"Lord Williamson wanted to kill him; you saw that too!" Rochelle replied. "I will not be the cause of trouble anymore. I'll leave today, and I'll return to my home."

"It is your decision to make, my dear," was all Lady Wright could say.

"Be aware that I will always be fond of Your Ladyship," Rochell informed her. Lady Wright hugged her, while Rochelle was moved.   Meanwhile, Christopher returned home, and decided to read the letters.Learning about the real nature of Rochelle's conversations with Lord Williamson, he was impressed by her words.

He realized what he had already sensed, that Rochelle was not the same as her brother and she had not been tempted by Lord Williamson's richness.

Could Rochelle have been the woman he had been looking for for so long? Did he have her before his eyes for all that time without realizing it? Had he been so blinded by being biased? ☐

Chapter 6

The following morning Christopher had the opportunity to converse with Rochelle, and he gave her back her letters.

"These belong to you," he said as he delivered it to her., "They are the letters that Lord Williamson returned yesterday."

"You took them?"Rochelle asked him in surprise.

"I thought you would have wanted them one day," Christopher replied.

"And... have you read them?"

"I know I should not have done it; I apologize."

Rochelle was uncomfortable, and she turned around without saying a word.

"Now I understand many things...," Christopher continued, but she intervened.

"Please, Sir Christopher. This is a question between me and Lord Williamson."

"Of course. I did not mean to be intrusive. It's just that I have realized that I have judged you too hastily. And I owe you an apology for this."

"You owe me nothing. I do not know you, and you do not know me."

"I do not mean to be bold. The thing is that I admired your strength in replying to Lord Williamson and in defending your honor,"

"Did you have a poor opinion of me, did you?" Rochelle asked, stunned by his words.

"I let myself be deceived by your brother's ambition. I do not mean to speak badly about him..." he started saying but Rochelle intervened.

"I am not my brother. And I have done nothing more than what I had to do."

"Not everyone is that steadfast. Many couples get married without the family's consent."

"Lord Williamson did not love me sincerely."

"Even if he did, it would not justify his behavior. The noblest feeling can turn into concupiscence."

"I agree. Besides, you do not need to worry about it anymore. I was told my brother will be back tomorrow. So I can return to my home."

"I am glad for you."

"Thank you for all you have done, Sir Christopher."

"Just call me Christopher. I hope we will keep our friendship."

"Of course. And I have promised your mother that I will come to visit you all."

Rochelle took leave and retired to her room to pack her baggage, helped by her maid.

About Lord Williamson, he had desisted from his purpose, wounded in his pride by the humiliation of the duel.

Later, it became known that he had obtained the annulment of his previous marriage and that he had married another woman.

When John Chapman returned to Dublin, he brought along his betrothed, along with her family. The Chapmans hosted them in their house, and Lady Chapman immediately loved the lady, Rose, who was a meek and educated young lady.

Lady Chapman informed John of what had happened during his absence. John was shocked and indignant in learning what Lord Williamson had done and, furious, he meant to ask him for satisfaction.

"He dared to disrespect Rochelle by doing such an indignity! He will answer for his actions," he promised.

"He has already been challenged for a duel by Sir Christopher," replied Lady Chapman. "The duel ended in a draw; they had injured each other."

"It is for me to defend Rochelle's honor, I am the householder," John replied. "And I can't just leave it."

"Do you want to fight him too?: Lady Chapman asked him. "What would it be the point? Just send him an indignant letter; it will be enough."

Lady Chapman managed to calm him down. In the afternoon, they went to fetch Rochelle at Wright mansion, and in the meanwhile, John told his mother that he had finally found a betrothed suitable for Rochelle. He was a Viscount, and he held a political office. He was about forty-five years old.

Arriving at Wright mansion, John and Lady Chapman had been received by the Wrights, and John saw Rochelle again. He thanked the Wrights and Christopher for their assistance.

"I thank Your Lordships for the hospitality you reserved for Rochelle. And for your assistance, of course, Sir Christopher. I have heard you saved Rochelle from unpleasant encounters twice."

"I just did what any gentleman had to do," Christopher replied.

"And I have also heard that you fought a duel with Lord Williamson to defend Rochelle's honor, which I would have done for myself if I was here," John replied. "This proves to me that you are a man of honor."

"I have great respect and a very high esteem for your family and for Miss Chapman," Christopher said. "She is a woman of great dignity and integrity. You must be proud of her."

"I am," John replied, smiling. Rochelle was impressed by Christopher's words.

When she accompanied her maid to the room to take the baggage, Rochelle met Christopher in the corridor.

"I was looking for you to talk," he said.

"Tell me, Sir," Rochelle replied.

"Did your brother mention in his letters about a betrothed for you?" Christopher asked.

"Why do you ask?" Rochelle asked, the question taking her by surprise.

"I know I do not have the right to do it… but if you agree, I would like to ask your hand in marriage,"

"I never thought that you…," she said in show, unable to finish the phrase.

"I have met many ladies in marriageable age during the Season, but none of them have half of your spirit," he informed her. "You are certainly the most noble person I have ever known,"

Rochelle was impressed, but she was confused at the same time and she did not know what to say.

"Just say if you would allow me to speak to your brother," Christopher continued. "If you believe you could correspond my feelings for you, Rochelle…"

She suddenly felt happy and nodded.

"You can speak to him," she whispered. Christopher smiled and took his leave.

He went into the hall while Rochelle was wondering about her feelings for Christopher. Her admiration for him had grown since he had defended her honor, risking his life... was there something more? And she soon began to hope for John to accept Christopher's proposal.

When Christopher joined the Chapmans, he asked to speak to John privately.

"I was informed about the reason for your journey out of town. This is why perhaps I should not be so conceited to make such a proposal. But in all this time, I have learned to know and to appreciate Rochelle. And I would like to ask for her hand in marriage."

John looked at him, bewildered into silent.

"I am not the richest in Society..." continued Christopher, "But I can offer a dignified life to Rochelle and my devotion."

"Did you fight with Lord Williamson because you wanted Rochelle for yourself?" John asked suspiciously.

"Of course not. I would have done it for any woman. And I can assure you that in all the time she spent here, I have always treated her with the utmost respect."

"You know, Mr. Wright, I have already refused many marriage proposals for Rochelle by wealthy and honored men. Rochelle deserves the best, and I am trying to provide it to her."

"I perfectly understand, but I would ask you to look beyond my status and consider my honesty and reliability."

"I am not questioning that you possess such virtues, Sir Christopher. But, with all due respect, those qualities do not improve the family's patrimony nor status. And besides, I have found a betrothed suitable for Rochelle."

Christopher was disappointed and didn't say anything.

"But I am grateful to you for what you did for Rochelle," continued John, and then he took his leave.

John called Rochelle and she said goodbye to Lady Wright and to Christopher, longing to learn about the conversation between Christopher and John.

"Did Sir Christopher tell you something about me?" Rochelle asked in the carriage.

"He did," John replied without looking at her. "But I could not accept his proposal."

Rochelle was visibly upset.

"What proposal?" Lady Chapman asked.

"Sir Christopher asked for Rochelle's hand in marriage."

"Did Sir Christopher intend to marry her?" Lady Chapman asked in surprise.

"Doesn't Christopher possess the right qualities for being

my husband?" Rochelle asked John.

"I do not question his morals. But he cannot offer you the position that you deserve."

"The position that I deserve, or maybe the one you're aspiring to?" Rochelled said with disappointment in her voice.

"Why are you talking to me in this way?"

"I do not mean to disrespect you, John. But don't you care about my happiness?"

"Of course I do, and which is why I have found a betrothed that is worthy of you."

Rochelle was bewildered, but did not reply.

"He is a Viscount and he will come soon to meet you," John continued.

Rochelle, saddened, said nothing,

"Won't you say thank you?" asked John.

"Of course," murmured Rochelle.

Back home, Rochelle wanted to retire in her room after welcoming Miss Rose and her folks and introducing herself to them. Rochelle could think of nothing but that she would not see Christopher again. That evening, she did not want to eat.

Lady Chapman realized that something was troubling her, and she suspected that it was something to do with Christopher. So she decided to talk to her.

"I was surprised to learn about Sir Christopher's proposal," she said. "I had no idea he was courting you."

"He wasn't," Rochelle replied. "I am surprised as much as you."

"Do you have feelings for him?"

"I admire Sir Christopher very much," she replied with awe in her voice.

"It is not what I meant. If you did not, you would not be so upset?"

"I am not upset, mother," Rochelle replied, uncomfortable at revealing her emotions. "It's just I don't even know who my betrothed is. I have learned to know Christopher, and I know he is a man of honor. I have seen his devotion to his family. I am certain he would be a good husband for me."

"We have to trust your brother, trust his judgment. You will get to know your betrothed pretty soon."

"Why won't you talk to John? He would listen to you. Please persuade him not to grant my hand in a frenzy."

"I think he would not accept my advice. But you don't need to worry about it; everything will be fine," Lady Chapman said, kissing Rochelle goodnight.

Meanwhile, Christopher was not much better than she was. All evening, he let his trouble out by boxing until exhaustion. His soul was in tumult; he didn't want to give up on Rochelle, but he didn't want to disrespect her family either.

The following day, Christopher suggested his mother visit Rochelle the day after.

In the meantime, Rochelle spent part of the day with Rose, trying to get to know each other. Rochelle tried to let her feel at home

"We shall be as sisters," she told her.

"I never had one. I would love to," Rose replied.

Rochelle realized the day had gone by without Christopher looking for her, and she was concerned. She was missing Wright mansion; she was missing the conversations with Lady Wright, and seeing Christopher every day.

But the following day, she was pleasantly surprised to receive Lady Wright's visit, and she welcomed her, conversing then with her.. She asked about Christopher.

"He is busy with his usual business," Lady Wright replied. "So, I have heard soon there will be a wedding in your family?"

"Indeed. I am so glad for my brother," Rochelle replied.

"Is there any other news?" Lady Wright asked.

"Well... no, not yet," Rochelle replied, preferring not to mention her betrothed. "My brother's journey hasn't been as successful as we had hoped. At least he has found his own betrothed."

"Don't be worried about it," Lady Wright replied. "He will

find a betrothed for you too, I am certain."

When it was time to leave, Lady Wright was fetched by Christopher, and Rochelle wasglad for his arrival. After greeting, she and Christopher accompanied Lady Wright to the carriage. Rochelle said goodbye to her, and Christopher walked Rochelle to the front door.

"I tried to convince your brother of my noble intentions towards you," Christopher told her.

"He wants me to marry a Viscount. He shall be here within a few days," Rochelle replied.

"Now that I found you, I do not want to lose you," Christopher whispered.

"Me either," Rochelle said. He kissed her on her cheek .

"You will hear from me again," he said, and they looked at each other with a hopeful look before Christopher walked away.

That afternoon, John was informed about Lady Wright and Christopher's visits, and he had more suspicions about the nature of the relationship between Christopher and Rochelle. He later questioned Rochelle about it.

"What kind of feelings do you really have for Christopher Wright?"

"I have a great admiration for Sir Christopher," Rochelle replied, surprised by the question. "He saved me, and he fought with Lord Williamson to defend my honor."

"Is that all?" John asked, revealing his suspicions. "Considering your reaction to my refusal, it seems to me there is something more."

"Sir Christopher has got virtues that I have never seen in other men," Rochelle replied, feeling uncomfortable.

"You do not know men, Rochelle. They can be persuasive when they want a woman."

"He has never attempted to exercise any persuasion on me."

"It is better so."

"And about their visit today, it was a courtesy visit by him and Lady Wright, who has always treated me as her own daughter in all the time I have spent with them."

"I see."

"Why don't you appreciate Sir Christopher? Because he is not rich enough?" "You know I have already promised your hand to the Viscount. Besides, marriages have the purpose of improving the status and the prosperity of families."

Disillusioned, Rochelle retired. But she was unaware that Christopher was going to speak to John again. The following day, he came and asked to be received by John.

Surprised by the visit but suspecting the reason why, John received him.

"What do I owe your visit to?" he asked him.,

"I dared to come to talk to you again, although you've already given a response to my proposal, to ask you to reconsider me as Rochelle's betrothed. I ask you to estimate my qualities and the sincerity of my feelings and not my position."

"Are you questioning my estimation ability?"

"It is not what I meant. I had the humility to lower myself to ask for a second time, despite knowing the little consideration you have of me."

"You are mistaken. On the contrary, I have a high consideration of you. You proved your worth by defending Rochelle. It's just that I don't believe you are suitable as a betrothed for her."

"I have never been ambitious, Mr. Chapman, and I never tried to improve my status or increase my family's patrimony. It is so because I dedicated myself to nurture qualities that matter most to me: discipline, obedience and honesty. And I don't have the presumption to say that I have fully pursued them. But I can assure you that my feelings for Rochelle are noblest.".

Rochelle surprised them by walking into the room, having overheard part of the conversation.

"Listen to him, John," she said. Rochelle had been Informed

of Christopher's visit, and she intended to support him.

"This is a matter between Sir Christopher and me," John said.

"It is right thath she takes part in our conversation," Christopher said. "She must know that I love her."

Rochelle was impressed with his response, sharing a soft smile.

"Do not try to charm her with words!", John said with a hostile tone, "I would never forgive you for such a baseness!"

"I have no intention of doing that," Christopher said.

"You are taking advantage of a young lady!"

"Don't underestimate Rochelle. She has already proven to be wise enough not to give into flattery. Otherwise, she would have already given into Lord Williamson's ones."

"Sir Christopher has always treated me with the due respect," Rochelle claimed. "He never took any liberties with me."

"It is better so. Besides, I am a man of my word, and I cannot back off from mycommitment to the Viscount. If you truly love her as you say, do not look for her again."

"I am not like Lord Williamson, you have nothing to fear from me," Christopher said, infuriated. He took his leave and walked away.

Rochelle was in grief, and she retired to her room and cried.

John preferred not to mention what had happened with his mother, and Rochelle did the same.

Rochelle was determined to do everything she could not to please the Viscount. Once he arrived there, she would make herself unpleasant in his eyes so that he would desist from marrying her. She did not speak to John for the following days except to greet him; aside from an evening when she and John were alone for some moments.

"I know you are angry with me," he said to her "But you will understand that everything I do is for your sake."

Rochelle was about to ignore him and to walk away when John continued.

"And if you are thinking of doing something reckless…"

"Christopher and I are not going to flee to get secretluyy married, as if we were criminals," Rochell quickly intervened. "I could have accepted Lord Williamson's proposal, but I did not, not to disrespect you and our family. And despite that, he had offered me richnesses and luxury I have. But you cannot renounce something out of your love for me."

With that said, she walked away.

In the following days, Christopher had his soul in torment. He had not spoken to anyone for days, not even with his folks. He boxd more than usual, several times in a day, until exhaustion set in. The Wrights sensed that something was wrong with him, but they never asked him about it, although they suspected that Rochelle was the reason for it.

Moreover, Christopher asked Lady Wright to abstain from visiting Rochelle for some time as not to cause her more friction.

Since he had dedicated his life to the pursuit of virtue, Christopher, although afflicted, knew deep in his heart that he had nothing to regret. The rectitude was the only richness that he valued and craved to possess.

☐

Chapter 7

Three weeks had passed since Rochelle's last encounter with Christopher, and she still had to meet her betrothed. He had written that he had been held back and he would arrive there soon.

Rochelle was still thinking of Christopher; he also had not stopped thinking of her, even though he never mentioned her name again, not even with Lady Wright.

It was a gloomy evening when John suddenly felt unwell. He had a fever. He thought it was a passing illness, but when he did not get better and he saw blood in the saliva, the doctor was called. John had contracted tuberculosis.

Concerned, the Chapmans provided him all the possible assistance. Lady Chapman and Rochelle prayed together in the evenings, and on an occasion, Rochelle spoke to her about him.

"I was so angry with him, but I would never wish him such a thing as that."

"Don't think about that," Lady Chapman replied.

Rochelle was in tears, but she was told by a servant that John had asked to speak to her.

Rochelle walked into his room, keeping her distance.

"You asked to speak to me?" she asked him.

"If I don't get better, I cannot leave you knowing you resent me," John said.

"Don't say that. You are going to recover," Rochelle said.

"I have to ask for forgiveness for me causing you grief," continued John.

"I forgive you with all my heart," Rochelle replied.

"I always cared about the family's welfare," John said after sighing.

"Don't think about it now, Rochelle comforted him. "Just think of regaining your strength."

"There is still a person I owe an apology to,…" John replied.

John sent for Christopher. Learning of the situation, Christopher was hesitant whether to comply with John's request or not, but Mr. Wright admonished him.

"Go and listen to what he has to say."

"I have already been humiliated enough by that man," Christpher responded.

"If you don't, you will regret denying him the chance to explain," Mr Wright advised.

Christopher realized that his father was right.

So the same day, he went to Chapman mansion, where he was received by Lady Chapman and Rochelle. He and

Rochelle looked at each other emotionally, and then she wanted to accompany him.

"I am very sad for your brother's illness," Christopher said.

"Thank you for coming. John would like to apologize to you," Rochelle told him. "A doctor is visiting for the moment."

"I can come back later," Christopher said.

"It is fine; it is almost done," Rochelle replied. "You can wait in the hall."

"I was thinking of not coming here," Christopher said shen they reached the hall. "I still have some resentment towards him."

"I truly understand," Rochelle commented.

"I was ungenerous, Christopher continued."

"You are here now," Rochelle said with a comforting smile.

"Maybe we should pray together for him to recover," he proposed. "Do you agree?"

"You are definitely the most decent person I have ever known," she said, nodding. "That is why I love you."

Christopher felt a sudden twinge of anguish, thinking he could not be with her.

Rochelle led him to the Chapel, and there they prayed together. When the visit was done, John received Christopher in his room.

"Thank you for coming," he said.

"You meant to speak to me?" Christopher asked him from a distance.

"During these days spent in this bed, I reflected on the things that you said to me, about the virtues you've tried to pursue. I understood that I do not possess them. I have been dedicated to keeping my family since my father died, and I have always believed I was doing well.

"But I have been overwhelmed after Rochelle's Debut; I used her as a means to improve the family's status."

Christopher listened to him carefully without saying a word.,

"Now I wish to be generous, for once in my life," John continued John. "Will you help me, Sir Christopher?"

"Help you?" Christopher asked "How could I?"

"Could you forgive me for my behavior?" John said.

"I am not so immodest to deny you my forgiveness," Christopher replied.

"Help me to act generously," he said in relief and then sent for Rochelle.

"You deserve a just and noble man as Sir Christopher is," John told her. "So I am entrusting you to him, confident that he will take care of you."

"Thank you, John," she said, smiling with teary eyes while

Christopher joyfully touched her hand.

Relieved of their pain, Rochelle and Christopher announced it immediately to Lady Chapman.

"John gave us his blessing," Rochelle said, Lady Chapman was surprised but glad for them.

"I am asking for your blessing, too, Lady Chapman," Christopher said. "I know I am not the betrothed you had hoped for Rochelle, but I can assure you of my dedication to her,"

"You are, indeed, sir Christopher," Lady Chapman replied. "You proved me your worth in more than one occasion. And I am glad for you both."

The pair rejoiced at Lady Chapman's approval, although they were still concerned about John.

Rochelle, Lady Chapman, and Rose supported each other in facing those difficult days. Rose, who feared losing her future husband before she could even marry him, gave him assistance with zeal, and Christopher, for his part, gave them his support and took John's responsibilities during his absence. Fortunately, John recovered, with the relief of the family.

When he got better, he asked to speak to Rochelle and Christopher; John showed them a letter.

"This is a letter addressed to the Viscount in which I

explain to him that I can no longer grant him Rochelle's hand in marriage. I further intend to go and speak to him face to face, as soon as I am able to, so I can apologize to him."

"I know it is not simple for you to back off your commitment," Rochelle replied. "But I thank you for making this decision."

"These are times of change," John continued. "I too wish to make changes in my life. I have been materialistic and selfish, but now I intend to nurture other values."

He then spoke to Christopher.

"Do you have any advice to share with me, Sir Christopher?"

"I don't think I am the right person to give advice, Sir John," Christopher replied, taken by surprise "The only thing I can tell you is that a start could be showing benevolence to poor ones."

"It is a good advice," John said.

John did his best to follow Christopher's advice.

About Christopher and Rochelle, that day, they went for a stroll in Chapman mansion garden.

"Thank you for not having openly defying John and not having turned against him," Rochelle said.

"How could you love me if I did?" replied Christopher. "Our union must be blessed, not illicit. You are dwelling in me."

He kissed her. Christopher and Rochelle then went to give the news to the Wrights, who were cheerful for them.

"I am pleased to have you as daughter," Lady Wright told her."You're welcome in our home."

"I am pleased too," Rochelled replied. "Your Ladyship has always been good to me."

"We could not hope for a better choice of you," Mr Wright said to Christopher, , giving them his blessing.

When it became known in Society that the "spearhead" of the Season, who had received over than one hundred marriage proposals, at last had chosen one of the less influent men, they began speaking of nothing but that for weeks.

The following week, Christopher and Rochelle officialized their engagement.

THE END